Gabrielle

By Albert Guerard

The Past Must Alter
The Hunted
Maquisard
Night Journey
The Bystander
The Exiles
Christine/Annette
Gabrielle

Gabrielle

An entertainment by
ALBERT GUERARD

DONALD I. FINE, INC.

New York

Copyright © 1992 by Albert Guerard

All rights reserved, including the right of reproduction in whole or in part in any form. Published in the United States of America by Donald I. Fine, Inc. and in Canada by General Publishing Company Limited.

Library of Congress Cataloging-in-Publication Data

Guerard, Albert J. (Albert Joseph), 1914-
   Gabrielle : an entertainment / by Albert Guerard.
      p. cm.
   ISBN 1-55611-288-2
   . I. Title
   PS3513.U353G3   1992   91-58663
   813'.52—dc20   CIP

Designed by Irving Perkins Associates

Manufactured in the United States of America

10   9   8   7   6   5   4   3   2   1

For
William Brewer
Robert Ergun
Russell Furbush

An American diplomat is seduced
into the midst of an amateur band
of kidnappers, lured by the be-
guilingly amoral and loveable
chambermaid at his Parisian hotel.

Sunday

Hotel Meurice

AT THIRTY-EIGHT THOMAS RANDALL WAS looked upon as a rising
young man, one who would go far. He was an outsider, but
his wife Roxanne was not. She had been in the Washington
establishment all her life, and she saw no reason why her
bright husband shouldn't go all the way. She furnished their
Georgetown house, saw to it that he wore the proper shirts
and ties, and guided him skillfully through the receptions.
Now, almost on the eve of the first international conference
he would chair, a Paris meeting on peace in Central America,
she wanted him to make the right impression on foreign
dignitaries. He had intended to stay at the Lutétia, where
the meetings would be held. He lived there through his four-
teenth year at a Paris lycée, often alone for winter weeks on

end when his widowed mother wandered off to Marrakech and other sunlit places. Nearby, for his free hours, were the heady turmoil and silken temptations of the Left Bank. Cabarets where even fourteen-year-olds were welcome.

But his wife Roxanne had other ideas.

"I want you to stay at the Meurice. A nice suite overlooking the Tuileries. You can have important people over for discreet talks. At the Lutétia the riffraff Latinos would try to corner you in the elevator. Make you look at petitions. You must keep your distance, be courteous but aloof. Someday you will be Secretary of State."

"Not very likely. Besides, they won't pay for it. What do you think an Assistant Secretary's per diem is? It might buy the bathroom of a Meurice suite."

"I have arranged to make up the difference."

"Have arranged?"

"I made the reservation yesterday. Believe me, you will love the Meurice. We always stayed there when traveling. Even mother's maid had a chambre de bonne in the hotel."

The Assistant Secretary remained silent. During this silence, and not for the first time, his nimble mind hovered over ideas of separation, divorce, flight. In the last minutes before sleep he sometimes regaled himself with fantasies of disappearance. To begin with a new name and clean slate, and no wife or department advisories or protocol to bind his arms!

For an outsider he had come a long way, from Berkeley and Georgetown Law School. His father, a dreamer and lawyer for lost causes, used to harangue the five- and six-year-old on their Sunday walks: lectured him on the duplicity and unctuous moralism of John Foster Dulles, Bundy and the rest. But the father died when the boy Thomas was thirteen, and the mother at once took him to Europe, and there spent much of their inheritance in the next two years. It was then he acquired the taste for travel that took him into the State Department by a back door. But he was amiable and intelligent, and got on well enough with the Harvards and Yales. He met and married the granddaughter of a senator, a graduate of Miss Porter's and Vassar. It was she who was ambitious as well as rich, he still hoped for travel and adventure.

A number of small parties over two years led to the department's discovery that it had, among its beginners, a talent worth nourishing. He was given opportunities, he fell into step. Slowly, almost insidiously, the cloak of the department's ideology settled about his shoulders. At first reluctantly, at last with conviction, he came to believe that trade depended on Order and Order depended on the cooperation of men, often generals, he would not want to share a desert island with.

And now he was Assistant Secretary of State for Hemisphere Cooperation! A new title but hardly a new job.

Occasionally, driving to his office in the department, he left his usual route to cruise slowly down a street of cafés and cantinas with Spanish names. The brassy music and glimpses of flashing teeth and bronze skin brought back nostalgically his first visit to El Salvador, Honduras and Nicaragua. Even then he only rarely could break away from the delegation for a few hours among the ordinary people. Secretly he preferred their laughing disorder to the oily courtesies of the colonels and the fawning intimacy of cabinet ministers. The liberalism of his college days was far behind but the instincts remained. He was the prisoner of his good marriage and his professional success.

In the last month before the Paris conference the noisy Latino protests multiplied. Poorly printed handbills bemoaned the State Department's historic support of the great landowners and its not so secret support of counterinsurgency police. Always the CIA worming its way along the corridors of power. The same posters and handbills appeared at the protests in Lafayette Park and on the steps of the Capitol. Thomas Randall made it a practice of accepting the handbills without breaking his stride or giving more than an impassive glance at the urgent brown faces crowded against the barrier. Always the same faces, or so it seemed.

One particular protester, however, made him pause. She was a young woman of perhaps nineteen, with regular features and luminous brown eyes set quite far apart. The two eyes appeared to converge not on his own eyes but on his mouth, as though hoping he would speak. Her exceptionally clean blouse had slipped off one shoulder to reveal olive skin of glowing softness. She thrust a document in his hands. He had a fleeting impulse to say something to justify the hard line he would have to take in the coming conference. And to tell her that he too felt compassion for the suffering of the shirtless ones. He too had protested in his time. He had even, his senior year at Berkeley, been arrested at a protest, though almost immediately released. Why hadn't the faculty gone on record against CIA intervention in Chile? Or perhaps it was Guatemala. How long ago that was.

He put the handbill in his pocket without inspecting it. But two days later, on his way to a subcommittee hearing in the Senate Office Building, he saw her again. She was near the head of a line of brown-skinned activists hoping for admission to the committee room. A bored policeman was making a halfhearted effort to keep them close to the wall. The woman's blouse had again slipped off her shoulder. Perhaps it was this that made him stop in his tracks, although to stop had certainly not been his intention. Their eyes met.

This time the exceptionally large and soulful eyes seemed to swim toward him, away from the rest of her face and body. Eyes in which two black dots were sunk in deep pools of brown. He wanted to say something that would convey his own outrage on behalf of the tortured and the starving. In another life they might have been friends, even lovers, he and this passionate young woman.

He found himself addressing her.

"I lost the paper you gave me the other day. Do you have another copy?"

Her mouth opened in astonishment. The teeth were regular and white, with almost no gold.

"You say?"

"The other day you gave me a handbill. I'm afraid I lost it."

Beside her a small protester was grinning. He addressed her in whispered Spanish so rapid that the Assistant Secretary caught not a word.

"Who are you, mister? What you want?" Her husky voice, though full of contempt, was richly enticing. "You are mister Randall, no? My friend say you are the evil Secretary."

Foolishly he persisted. He ventured his rusty Spanish.

"Quiero hablar contigo. Quiero explicar. After the hearing?"

He looked away from her relentless gaze. There was more rapid whispering, also nervous laughter. Involuntarily his eyes fell again to the bare shoulder and its brown softness, then to the line of protesters behind her, where several men were laughing. Thus he was not prepared for her swift feline movement, her step back and swift inrush of breath, and the quick thrust forward as she spat. A fine spray clung to his cheek.

The policeman, whose back must have been turned, was aware that something had happened. He approached. But

Randall waved him off. He was enraged at the laughter of her companions but did not want the young woman arrested.

"It's nothing. Just a little accident."

At the meeting, facing the senators and with his back to the audience as he testified, he was acutely aware of the woman, who had found a seat in the last row. He raised his voice, hoping she would hear. Fragile democracies require foreign investment and foreign investment demands Order, even a well-disciplined military. He wanted her to understand the administration's good intentions.

That night he went through the scatter of his papers. In the hip pocket of another pair of trousers (his wife insisted he change frequently) he found the lost handbill. A crudely printed census of the number of women raped in each of the Central American republics, and of the husbands and sons and fathers who had been "disappeared." The handbill was signed by an Asociación de Mujeres, with an address in an area where houses were boarded up.

The next morning he drove past the association's address, which appeared to be combined bookstore, novelty shop and delicatessen, not more than twenty feet wide. Even from his car he could see that the many paperback books in the window looked worn. Biographies of Che Guevara and Castro, no doubt. Other sacred Marxist texts. Comic books in Spanish. Faded *piñatas* hung from the ceiling, just inside the door.

On second thought he decided there would be no use trying to establish further contact with the woman who spat on him. But it was saddening to think that she would never understand him and that he would never even know her name.

*   *   *

THE ASSISTANT SECRETARY LOOKED DOWN with longing on the Tuileries gardens, where there would be Sunday lovers in the summer twilight.

Twenty-four hours of unexpected freedom lay before him because the conference on Central America had been delayed: the small yet crucial meeting where he would again convey Washington's high moral outlook and firmness of will. A frustrated coup in Honduras had caused the delay; a new delegation had to be appointed.

Tomorrow afternoon at the reception for delegates he would be "himself," the controlled master, indicating by warm or perfunctory handshake the degree of Washington's approval or disapproval. And his would be, Tuesday morning, the dominant voice at the roundtable. But tonight he longed to wander again the Paris of his lycée year at fourteen. There would be a sidewalk café on the *boule miche*, his eye out for a pretty barefoot student cadging a few francs or a meal, miniskirts and earrings that reached bare shoulders. Except there was always the possibility of recognition by some strolling journalist or American professor on sabbatical. So it would have to be instead a modest dinner in a working-class district, Belleville or near the Bastille, magret de canard perhaps and a good Chambertin or Pommard. Then to wander wherever his feet led him, and some still unknown companion for the night.

Twenty-four hours, all of Paris in his hands—except for the two dullards assigned to protect him. One or the other would always be watching from a strategic corner of the gilded lobby from which both public entrances could be observed. One entrance on the rue de Rivoli, the other on the rue Mont Thabor with its porte-cochère from the great times. The vanished years when only the Meurice would do for reigning or deposed kings.

And of course one of the two men would want to accompany him on his wandering. Unthinkable for an Assistant Secretary of State to stroll the rue Royale or the Boulevard des Capucines unattended, let alone the dark streets off the rue St. Denis or the Place Pigalle! Especially an Assistant Secretary whose official persona was feared and hated by so many throughout the long dark curve of turmoil and subversion, from Panama to Matamoros, not to mention the angry exiles in Miami, Santo Domingo, even Paris. How many men of his age could arouse the same visceral response in Managua and Tegucigalpa and San Salvador and Port-au-Prince? The thought gave him no pleasure. He liked to be understood. How little they understood his good intentions!

There could be French journalists in the lobby too, not only the security men. Or, worse still, members of his own or another delegation. *We have a table at the Tour d'Argent, one more is no problem, of course you must join us, Randall, not very nice to block incoming calls.* Preferable to that would be dinner in his room and the slow diminution of a good bottle, a careful honing of his Tuesday speech, knowing the phone would not ring. A lost evening and hole in time, while the golden roar and silvery summer twilight of Paris went on without him, and the crowded cafés of midnight.

A hole in time, twenty-four hours that for his superiors need not exist. His eyes followed the game, beneath the Tuileries wall, of a jaunty blonde with black boots up to the thigh and a sullen poodle on leash. The dog was her pretext for turning to see who was following her, in this instance a timid middle-aged tourist. The Assistant Secretary imagined himself in the tourist's place, and the woman's surprise at his good French. Distracted, all but hidden between the folds of curtain and the window, he was not even aware that the maid had knocked, had come in, and was already folding back the bedcover rich as a Gobelin tapestry. Sheets of gossamer softness and pillows worthy of the pink nubile Boucher maiden reclined on a love seat above his bed, her glowing forearms resting on rosy satin puffs. An immense bed, where Edward VII himself might have disported with a splendid courtesan on each flank and a third rubbing his toes. The three would be clothed in black stockings. Only that.

The maid worked swiftly and silently. A cool smile to acknowledge his presence: she could see he was a thinking man, not to be disturbed.

He scrutinized her as she stroked and patted the pillows: a crisp efficient Molière soubrette, rather than a Boucher adolescent. Twenty-four or five, small-breasted, firm and sleek of limb, almond lightly waving hair under her small provocative cap, a uniform that would be soft and cool to the touch. Soulful Parisian eyes, even though he couldn't see them yet, a mouth made for ironic ripostes or slow yet audacious caresses. At the thought of such caresses, the long tongue and teeth, his own flesh slowly, then firmly responded. She would be restless as a cat in bed, very firm of muscle, capable of biting if angry.

But now he could see the brown eyes, since she had looked up from her labors and was staring at him appraisingly.

"Monsieur desires something?"

At an airport hotel in Los Angeles or Miami, with a brown Latina face looking up from the bed, and many golden teeth, such a question could mean much. *Monsieur desires something else?* In the Sheraton in Salvador or Tegucigalpa, the Intercontinental in Managua ... But not, surely, in the Hotel Meurice! All he really wanted was to touch the crisp black skirt or the jaunty cap, just one playful squeeze of buttock.

At the same time, in a deeper stratum of desire, he boiled with rage, remembering a hotel maid in Tegucigalpa who had led him on. An evening that left him with his thirst.

"Thank you, no." But would this quintessential Parisian maid, correct yet perhaps available, dare to take five or ten minutes off and accept a drink? "Yes, of course I desire something. At least I'd like to drop in at Maxim's for a cocktail, then stroll along the boulevards, all the way to the Bastille."

"Why not? Maxim is only two hundred meters. For the Bastille I advise a taxi."

"I have problems."

She evaluated him unblinkingly. The brown eyes, a lovely mouth, two horizontal lines of thought.

"Problems?"

The bed remained between them. She had not moved to the bathroom, though a mound of fresh towels awaited her. He pointed to his bottle of Scotch.

"May I offer you something?"

Her laugh was not unfriendly. Her manner was, simply, "correct."

"Thank you, monsieur. It's not permitted." She looked at and past him, soulfully, a stage stare. "Everyone has problems."

"My problem is that I don't want to spend the evening with my American companions. They'll probably want to go to the Lido or the Crazy Horse."

"You don't like that kind of spectacle?"

"I don't like being surrounded by Americans on my one free evening in Paris. I like speaking French. I was a student here, at the lycée when I was fourteen."

"Which lycée?"

"Condorcet."

"Really? That is one of the best. It is for the bright boys. Also for the rich."

The silence returned, persisted. Was she after all available, though not perhaps at once? At least she seemed intelligent, she would understand his desire for a quiet evening speaking only French, or speaking not at all, just strolling, just following his nose.

"What's your name?"

She hesitated. Would she make up a name? What name would he himself use for a twenty-four hour indiscretion?

"Gabrielle."

"That's a nice name. So, Gabrielle—do you think you could smuggle me out of the hotel this evening so I won't have to be with my American friends? So I can have an evening by myself in Paris? There must be a service elevator, also a service entrance. I don't want to be seen by anyone in the lobby."

She was thinking hard. Her eyes fell, involuntarily fixed themselves in the area of his hip, where there would probably be a wallet. Or perhaps voluntarily.

"Naturally I would want to recompense you."

She frowned, raised her hands in protest, shrugged, acquiesced.

"I will see what is possible, monsieur. At eight o'clock I leave the hotel. Will that be too late? If possible I will arrange for a friend to come with a taxi to meet us at the service entrance." She measured him coolly. "With my good friend."

Never mind: there were other fish in the sea. His erection, moreover, had already subsided. It would be enough, just to stroll quietly in the warm Paris night, or take cover in a bright café if a sudden shower should occur.

"Of course," he said, "With your good friend."

"And what is your name, monsieur?"

For a moment he thought of saying *Elliott Abrams*. Or why not *George Schultz*, footloose in Paris? Certainly not his own name, Thomas Randall. A name came to him out of the deep past.

"Alger Hiss."

The Assistant Secretary with the infamous spy's name as a cover. Why not?

"I will come for you at eight o'clock, unless that is impossible, to take you out by the *sortie de service*. If impossible I will telephone you, Monsieur Iss."

"You can't phone because the phone is blocked."

She looked at him with renewed interest. The calculating scrutiny few French women can conceal, no more than they can conceal the instant inspection of one's shoes.

"Ah? Very well, monsieur. I will come for you myself, whether it is possible or not. To your door. I knock twice. Then you know it is me, Gabrielle."

THE GUARD AT THE SERVICE entrance was preoccupied by a ringing phone. They stepped past unseen. At once a nearby taxi dipped its lights, then moved toward them. Behind it two limousine taxis waited near the entrance to the curving porte-cochère. Their yellow lights were dimmed. The Assistant Secretary followed the maid Gabrielle, appraising her bare legs and sandals and white pleated skirt, already enjoying the unchanged smells of the Paris night, although the strident horns of his lycée year were gone. The great city was his for the asking!

She opened the door for him and insisted that he get in first. Almost pushed him in.

"It is the monsieur I spoke of. He wants to see Paris. For

the moment he wants to get away from the hotel and his American friends.''

The driver shrugged.

''It's none of my business what monsieur desires. On the other hand, if he desires to see Paris, I am an expert. Which Paris? Paris erotic or Paris artistic? The night clubs, Notre Dame, Montmartre?''

''Shut up,'' Gabrielle said. ''Monsieur does not want to be followed. Let's go!''

The taxi coughed, staggered forward, slid off into darkness.

''No one's going to follow me,'' the Assistant Secretary said. ''I just wanted to get out of the hotel without being seen. Drop me off anywhere.''

''Why did you say your name was Iss?'' Gabrielle asked. ''There is no Iss in the hotel. In fact there is no name in the list for your room. I have my good friend at the desk who told me.''

''It's of no importance. It was a joke. For one night I want to be Monsieur Anonymous.'' He patted a silken knee; it did not move away. ''Your good friend at the desk? In the U.S. it all depends on how you say it, 'my friend' or 'my good friend'. It depends on the tone of voice.''

''In France also.''

The driver accelerated, turning onto the Boulevard Malesherbes. Without signaling he left it and shot off into a dark side street, leaving the streaming lights of the boulevard.

''What's the matter?'' Gabrielle asked.

''There is a taxi that follows us. Since the hotel.''

She turned to look, Randall also turned to look. There were yellow headlights perhaps a hundred yards back in the long narrow street. But his protectors would still be seated in the lobby, waiting for his instructions. No one would be following.

"Where do you want to go, monsieur? You desire a good quiet restaurant?"

"First a room in a quiet hotel away from the tourists. Then a good restaurant near the Bastille."

"You do not return to your room in the Meurice?"

"Not tonight."

"*Attention*!" the driver said urgently. "We're taking off."

A wild squeal of tires, a wrenching under the ribs as the taxi swung into another dark street. They seemed to be going in circles, but faster and faster. Back onto the Boulevard Malesherbes.

"What is it? What's the matter?"

"We are certainly being followed, monsieur. But do not concern yourself, we will take you to a safe place."

"But that's crazy. There's no way anyone could be following me."

"Nevertheless there is a taxi following. We will go to the Bon Accueil. Not a two-star hotel, no stars at all. But there monsieur will be safe."

"I'm perfectly safe," the Assistant Secretary said. "Just drop me off at the next corner. No, take me to the Grand Hotel."

Gabrielle's cool hand, but a hand that at once became hot, squeezed his reassuringly. But firmly.

"That would not be possible, monsieur."

"Why not?"

"You asked for my help. I am giving you my help. I cannot abandon you to a danger that is not known."

"Just let me pay you now," Randall said. "How much do you want?"

Were these people trying to hustle him to an underground club where he could be rolled fifty dollars for a warm glass of champagne? Even worse things might happen.

"It's not for money, monsieur. It is for friendship I am helping you. Later, if you wish to make a little present, that would be nice."

The driver accelerated again.

"The dirty type is still following us," he said. "The cunt."

Even the intonation had not changed since the courtyard chatter of the Lycée Condorcet a quarter of a century before: *Le sale type nous suit toujours. Le con.*

The Bon Accueil was not a hotel, not even a *maison de passe*. A narrow doorway wedged between the glittering lights of a Sex Shop and a small bar. A woman wearing only fishnet stockings, tight shorts and a bra of billowing black silk watched him noncommitally from the door of the bar. There were few other lights on the narrow street which, to judge from its slow rise, must be somewhere above St. Lazare on the slope leading to the Place Clichy. "This way, monsieur, quick!" The driver, abandoning his taxi to the care of Gabrielle, guided Randall very firmly up a corkscrew stairway to a third floor room that had no window. An unmade single bed, a small television set and VCR, an armchair with protruding springs, a desk on which someone had been making computations. A hand-lettered sign on the door warned *locataires* not to feed their animals on the stairs, and to depose their ordures in the courtyard *poubelle*. The room, he surmised, was the bachelor dwelling of the taxi driver, who had introduced himself as Luc. There was a chamber pot under the bed. Through thready curtains, however, he could see the dull glow of a toilet without a seat. Above it was a small window from which, perhaps, one could see the street and even call for help. On the wall there was, thank God, a telephone. But what good was a telephone if, even going to the toilet, he was not alone?

The Assistant Secretary was terrified.

"Here you will be safe, monsieur. Only an hour or so, not more, then we will take you to a better hotel. Wherever you wish."

"I want to go to the Grand Hotel right now. I will pay you—"

"Who spoke of money? Any friend of Gabrielle is a friend of mine."

As though in response to her name, Gabrielle came into the room and sat down on the bed. She evidently had her own key, with which she now relocked the door. Randall found himself guided to the armchair by the driver Luc, who sat down on the desk. From this elevation Luc could, as it were, take command.

"We are glad to be of help, monsieur. But I ask you in all sincerity: Why are you being followed?"

"I'm not being followed."

"Important men of affairs are often followed without their knowing it. It is of interest to ask who they meet. What do they buy or sell? Why does an important man of affairs choose to evade his friends waiting for him in the lobby of the Hotel Meurice? Why does he ask a trusted employee of the hotel to take him out the service exit? Any client of the Hotel Meurice is an important man of affairs. What are your affairs, monsieur?"

The voice of Luc had become delicately aggrieved, as though Randall's behavior was unreasonable, even unfair.

"I am an ordinary tourist who wants to revisit the Paris of his student days."

Gabrielle scratched herself lazily, without pretence, as though he were already a good friend. Scratched under one armpit, then under the other.

"Tomorrow, which is my day off, I will personally take you to visit the Lycée Condorcet. One of the best lycées of

Paris, that is well known." She was still friendly, but her eyes seemed to be changing color, from brown to a milky gray. An illusion cast by the single naked bulb that hung quite low, like a weapon, he thought.

"I would be happy to accompany you anywhere tomorrow," Randall said. "But tonight I want to go to a good hotel. In fact I want to go back to the Meurice. There I can pay you a reasonable sum for your trouble. My money is in the hotel safe, not in my room."

Both the driver Luc and Gabrielle laughed. Then Luc:

"You were going to wander about Paris without money! What do you take us for?" His tone became less friendly. "Show me your passport." A *tutoiement,* as though their relations had changed. *Montre ton passeport!*

Randall turned his coat pockets inside out, then held the coat open as to invite a further inspection. It had, of course, been an essential condition of his twenty-four-hour hole in time: to go out with only a blank sheet of hotel stationery in case of accident. No name, only a room number. And three hundred dollars in hundred franc bills. He took the bills from his hip pocket. In doing so he dislodged a small packet of condoms that fell to the floor.

Gabrielle laughed and clapped her hands. She picked up the condoms and inspected the package. Read a few words in schoolgirl English.

"So monsieur wants to amuse himself? Bravo! Luc can make any arrangements you wish."

"And no credit card?" Luc asked. "That is folly, monsieur, unbelievable folly. I think in another pocket you have a credit card and perhaps a driver's license. No?"

"You're free to look. Especially since you're going to anyway."

"Let me see what you have," Luc said. He leaned forward,

appeared to leap the ten feet or so of intervening space, and seized the fresh hundred franc bills. Fresh because provided by his Washington office, which already seemed to him to be on another planet. Luc counted the bills, licking his thumb, then returned them with a little expletive of contempt. Like a fart issuing from puckered lips. A very French expletive.

"Be polite, Luc."

"But how can we protect monsieur if he doesn't help us or help himself?"

"Go down to the bar and get us some beer, Luc. Will you have a beer, monsieur?"

"Yes, in the bottle."

Luc closed the door, locking it behind him. Gabrielle offered an apologetic, even ingratiating smile.

"He is a fool, a retarded who keeps bad company. You must forgive his way of speaking. He doesn't know how to talk to a client of the best hotel in Paris. He sees you only as a man in danger, like a gangster."

"If you will just help me..."

"I am trying to help you, monsieur. Monsieur what? Not, I think, Monsieur Iss."

Was it too late to come up with a more plausible name? Probably.

"Alger Hiss was a famous traitor, long ago. I just happen to have the same name."

"How do you spell 'Alger'?"

"A-l-g-e-r. The same as the city in North Africa. In English Algiers. A-l-g-i-e-r-s."

"And 'Iss'?"

"H-i-s-s. Pronounce the 'h'."

"As for me: Gabrielle. Gabrielle Soubiran. S-o-u-b-i-r-a-n."

"It's very important for me to get back. You are an intelligent young woman. Surely you see there's nothing to be
had from me here. Only these few francs. But in the hotel,
once I get access to the hotel safe..."

"But think of me, monsieur Hiss! I am an employee of
the Hotel Meurice, a position I do not wish to lose. Surely
you see I too have problems! I had no idea you would be
followed by men in another taxi, terrorists no doubt. And
now my friend is causing problems. He is acting in a very
strange manner, so to speak. I had no idea he would behave
in this manner. You saw yourself."

She patted the bed beside her, not really to invite him, or
not for the moment, since Luc would soon return, but only
to say that she regretted everything. A misfortune, that she
had tried to help him.

"I assure you I will say nothing at the hotel," Randall said.
"If you take me back. Now, at once."

"You must arrange things with Luc, monsieur. I am only
a poor femme de chambre."

Luc returned with three bottles of beer, two of them in
his coat pockets. And with a Polaroid camera.

"Where did you get that?" Gabrielle asked.

"From the Sex Shop."

"You know how to use it?"

"Of course." He addressed Randall without looking up
from the camera. "It would be simpler if monsieur were to
identify himself without delay. And explain what he is doing
in Paris. And why he is being followed."

"Let's drop the pleasantry of my being followed."

He had, somewhat to his own surprise, adopted the impatient tone of an Assistant Secretary, himself, Thomas Randall, dealing with an evasive figurehead, a Guatemalan
diplomat perhaps. Or Costa Rican.

Luc put the camera down. A commanding gesture, almost a slapping gesture, indicated to Randall that he was to get up and follow him through the curtain to the toilet. And to stand on the toilet, look out the small window. To stand on tiptoe in fact.

"You see the taxi? The limousine taxi."

"I don't see a taxi."

"It will be back, no doubt. It is the dirty type that followed us from the Meurice. Two men in fact."

The Assistant Secretary stepped down from the toilet.

"You set them up. Arranged for them to follow us. Maybe there wasn't any taxi. What kind of idiot do you take me for?"

"Let us keep the conversation friendly," Luc said. "Just tell who you are and why you are in Paris and why your name is not on the register of the Hotel Meurice. Sit down on the bed."

"Alger Hiss, tourist. ASN 31361598."

"What is that?"

"My army serial number."

"You are a maker of farces, monsieur. You want to play games? Listen to me. You want to see Paris? I will bring Paris to you. Which do you want, a boy or a girl? Two of each? A woman with a whip? A dancer in the costume of a nun? Just indicate your preference."

Randall decided to ignore this, although Luc's tone was friendlier.

"It would be better to cooperate," Gabrielle said. "Soon we will both be back in the Meurice. All this will arrange itself."

"That's enough chatter," Luc said. "I'll have to take the pictures. It won't take long to find out who we have here, playing games with our good intentions. Sit on the bed, monsieur.''

In the first picture, which he too was allowed to look at, he had the appearance of a degenerate because of the unmade bed.

"What are you going to do with the pictures?'' Gabrielle asked.

"Find out who he is, our stubborn friend. François will know.''

"Who is François?'' Randall asked.

"A journalist.'' Luc tapped the camera as though it were an obedient dog. "If necessary there will be more pictures. Better ones. Group pictures with young ladies from the Sex Shop, why not?''

Candid Camera

Fortunately the small rue de Berri bar frequented by journalists was almost empty at this hour. At a table near the door two men in turtleneck sweaters were loudly discussing a new movie, otherwise the place was quiet. As far away from them as possible the taxi driver Luc, who felt uncomfortable in these surroundings, waited for his friend the sportswriter François. Once or twice a month he bought François drinks and paid him for information on coming events. If a boxer was concealing broken ribs or a tennis star was cracking up or an unknown foreign cyclist might win the Tour de France, François would know. He had many connections.

François entered the bar, greeted the bartender, and sat down opposite Luc. He was all of sixty and of the epoch when handshaking was obligatory. Not exactly a claw, more like the hand of a dead person, cold and hard. His face was narrow and leathery, with the pockmarks of a *nordafricain*. Something in the sharp inquisitive eyes reminded Luc of his American in the Bon Acceuil. His "prisoner," his "hostage"? Such words should be avoided.

"Tell me right away what you want at this hour of the night."

"Have something first. A cognac?"

"I haven't the time."

Luc took the photographs from his coat pocket and pushed them across the table, one by one.

"You know everybody. Who is he, this American?"

François spread the six pictures as for a game.

"He looks rather sick. What is he doing on your bed?"

"It's not my bed," Luc said prudently. "Someone else's."

"What is he selling? I see you don't trust him."

"I just want to know who he is."

François would have recognized at a glance the swollen nose and missing teeth of any well-known boxer, past or present. Or the transfixed stare of a black African distance runner of Olympic stature. But he rarely looked at the political pages. He would have recognized the Giscards and the Mitterands, but not the latest German or Greek statesman indicted for corruption.

"Why?"

"He insulted Gabrielle. I think he owes her an apology. And compensation."

"He's a client of the Meurice?"

"I didn't say that."

"So where did he insult her, your American, if not at the hotel?"

"Come on, François. Do you know this face? They are not

unknowns, the rich ones who stay at the Meurice."

"I agree that he looks familiar." He picked up the photographs, shuffled them, laid them out again. "A financier, perhaps. A millionaire, no doubt. Watch out, Luc. This is not a game for amateurs."

It was a conclusion Luc had already reached. But he was in it, the game, the stupid Gabrielle had got him into it. And a millionaire does not come along every day.

"You could go to the files at your paper. Why not?"

"Maybe tomorrow."

"It can't wait. I have to know who he is right away. Tonight."

"How much is it worth to you?"

"You're my pal, François," Luc complained. "Have I ever failed you? Let's say ten percent of whatever I get. The ten percent to include your expenses."

"Ten percent of nothing is nothing. What is ten percent of ten years in prison?"

"Okay. So we just let him go? Let him walk back to the hotel? Listen, he had two thousand francs on him. You can have them. A down payment."

The wiry face of soiled leather was aloof and contemplative.

"I don't mess with this sort of thing. Never. Keep your two thousand francs. For the moment, anyway. I will not meddle in this except to find out who he is. If I can. I'll call Georges Langlade who works for the *Express*. He will know. If he wants to come out at this hour."

"We can always go to him."

"He wouldn't like that. Not at all."

Georges Langlade was English, very British though French by birth. He had established his best contacts centuries before in Southeast Asia, where his calm demeanor and correct though drawling French succeeded in salons and offices many correspondents never reached. It was known that he had been parachuted into Cambodia but not known what he did there. Was he, through all his journalistic years, secretly serving British if not French intelligence? So it was rumored. His slow puffing of a pipe, and the way he fondled it, gave an impression of infinite wisdom.

At sixty-five, or perhaps more, he could still be brought away from his slippers and television by curiosity. He had a knack for knowing, instantly, when there was more to a story than his informants implied. So tonight he came to the bar where Luc and François were sitting.

He scrutinized the photographs noncommitally, then the faces of the two ingnoramuses: the sportswriter and his friend the taxi driver. Not an eyebrow moved. A leisurely puff on the pipe before removing it.

"Of course I know who he is. Why do you want to know?"

"Then he is that rich? Who is he?"

"All in due time. First understand that my only interest is in exclusive rights to the story. I never intervene. I do not make events, I report them." He picked up a photograph in which the subject's mouth was open, as in protest. "What is he doing on a bed that is obviously not a hotel bed? Whose bed is it?"

"Mine," Luc admitted. "He came to me for protection."

Now the ghost of a smile. Langlade was incapable of laughter.

"That is undoubtedly the craziest lie I ever heard. Next time maybe it will be the President of the United States who comes to you for protection?"

Luc stared.

"That is to say, he took my taxi and my taxi was followed by another one. Somebody who wants his money, no doubt.

But we gave them the slip. I am protecting him, this American."

"So he just flagged you down in the street or perhaps came to you because your taxi was the first in line? Excellent. Now me tell the truth."

"He insulted Gabrielle so I thought it necessary to teach him a lesson. And to demand on her behalf a small compensation."

"Gabrielle?"

"My girl. She is a femme de chambre in the Hotel Meurice. He insulted her when she was cleaning his room."

"Good. She will certainly not have to clean any more rooms in the Hotel Meurice. Maybe a cell in Fresnes, but not in any luxury hotels. Ever. The man you have kidnapped is the American Secretary of State for Hemisphere Cooperation. To be more accurate, Assistant Secretary of State. His name is Thomas Randall."

"My God!" François stood up. He waved a soiled finger at Luc. "You cretin! You get me in this mess and try to buy me for a few thousand francs. Call up Gabrielle and tell her to let the *sal type* out."

"Not so fast," Langlade said. He tapped the table with his pipe as to command total attention. "Never make precipitous decisions. For instance, what will your girlfriend say to the police who will take about ten minutes to find her? She has already lost her job, but that is only the beginning. What will the police say to you?"

"In other words?"

"I never give advice unless asked. But anyone can see it would be dangerous, more than dangerous, just to turn him out on the street. It is you who need protection, not the American diplomat. I never take money for advice, that must be quite understood. All I want is to know what happens.

Eventually I will want an interview, but by telephone. Is there a telephone in this miserable room?"

"Yes."

Luc found his confidence returning. An Assistant Secretary of State!

"It could mean millions. A bagatelle for the rich Americans."

"Don't think such thoughts," Langlade said. "Certainly not aloud. In the first place the American government would not pay a cent. Your problem is to contact someone who will take the risk of arranging for his safe release. Some organization."

"And who will pay me for the pains I have taken?"

Langlade sought solace in his pipe, and the silence it authorized. The moment was critical. There would be no story if Randall were simply bundled into a taxi and sent back to the Meurice. Only the comic anecdote of two ruined innocents, three if one included François. It was essential for him to have the full story of the kidnapping, beginning with the stupid taxi driver and his girlfriend, passing through many complications, and concluding with the released hostage at a press conference in the Embassy. Yes, end with the Assistant Secretary's release safe and sound, thanks to *his* prudent management of the affair. Langlade did not covet the praise of a grateful Embassy, certainly would not touch any hostage money. But he would have his story. This in fact could be the thorniest part of his task, to negotiate discreetly the right terms with an editor, possibly Berlin if London and New York wouldn't play.

He reflected nostalgically on the warm bed he had, for this night at least, left behind.

"Randall must be put in responsible hands. This is not a small affair."

"Surely someone will pay me for protecting him?"

"Possibly. But certainly not the U.S. government." Langlade relit his pipe with irritating slowness. He had the air of a man picking up, after a long vacation, a job he enjoyed. "The first thing you should know is that your American guest is in Paris for a conference on Latin America that begins Tuesday morning. A quiet conference in a private mansion on the boulevard . . . Never mind what boulevard. Tomorrow night there will be a reception at the Lutétia. No doubt there will be manifestations in the street. There are plenty of communist exiles in Paris who would love to see Randall squirm. Anticommunist exiles too."

"Is he such a monster?"

"Not necessarily. It's the State Department they detest but must bow down to. Even the little consuls of the Central American regimes in their walkup flats, and the shaky colonels sent by their bosses to cut the best deal they can. You understand? There is no one, right or left, the State Department has not at one time betrayed. That is what is called looking after one's interests. The fact remains that the betrayed sometimes have no choice. They must go along with Washington. And under certain circumstances the betrayed would pay for Randall's release, even though they'd love to see him rot in a room like yours."

"And so?"

"Of course none of that is what the Americans call real money. The real money is in Colombia. Or the PLO, Libya, Lebanon. There will be vultures everywhere asking themselves, 'Who has the Assistant Secretary? How can I get my hands on him?' "

"Vultures," Luc muttered. He looked at François accusingly. "I don't like what this Englishman is saying."

"I think you get the point. Your job is to get your guest

into responsible hands and protect your own withdrawal from the affair."

"You will intervene to make the necessary contact? We don't know these people."

Langlade tapped the table with his pipe. Three times.

"I never intervene. All I want is a good story with photographs. You need a good professional who can take pictures worthy of *Stern* or one of the London weeklies."

"My apartment is over a Sex Shop," Luc said. "No problem getting better pictures. But if you won't help us . . ."

"I will put you in contact with my dentist."

"Dentist!"

"Carlos Monzon, a Cuban, very rich. He has spent most of his life attacking Castro. There are few Paris or New York offices to compare with his suite on the Avenue Montaigne. X-ray machines worthy of *Star Wars*. A hygienist who caresses as she probes, with soothing words in Spanish. All the rich exiles go to Dr. Monzon, communists and ultraright alike. I believe your affair is sufficiently important for us to disturb him at this hour."

"You'll come with us?"

Langlade pointed the pipe at Luc. A very small weapon.

"No. I will make the contact. You will go back to your guest and assure his comfort. I'll take François with me." He stood up: the experienced officer in command. "I will do everything in my power to keep you and your girlfriend out of prison. Without intervening, of course."

BACK AT THE BON ACCEUIL, Luc found Randall and Gabrielle sitting side by side at the end of the small bed, which was still unmade, watching a film on the VCR. It had evidently come from the Sex Shop. Several naked men and a laughing

young woman were diligently at work. Their activities con-
firmed an intention Luc had toyed with earlier in the evening.

"The Englishman advises us to get better pictures," he
said.

Carlos Monzon

The awakened dentist, though immensely rich, opened the
door himself. His olive face, the late evening stubble heavily
powdered, revealed irritation tempered by curiosity and
greed. He had the look of a man taken rudely away from
some enjoyable but suspect pursuit. He was wearing a fur-
lined robe embossed with golden silk thread, a heavy yet
extraordinarily soft robe that reached his feet, which were
bare. The nails had not been cut.

"A robe copied from one much beloved by the novelist
Balzac," he offered, though no one had asked. He hesitated
before shaking hands with François. He was deterred by the
sportswriter's look of deprivation. Why had Langlade
brought such an underling?

Behind the dentist stretched a marble corridor from which
doors opened onto rooms filled with gleaming machines for
the tooth and jaw. They followed him to a reception room
decorated in immaculate Louis XVI. Love seats, armchairs
with golden silk, *grandes bergères* for dowagers. There were
tables with magazines concerned with antiques and expensive vacations. Also crisp news magazines in Spanish, French
and English. Even his richest clients came to the office. But
he was willing, for a first inspection, to cross the street to
patients' bedrooms in the Plaza Athénée. And once a month
he traveled to a small village south of Paris, La Morinière,

to treat the few terrible remaining teeth of a wealthy Haitian, Hypollite Jasmin, once the right-hand man, or almost the right-hand man, of the exiled Baby Doc. Monzon would go as far as Tangier to drill the tooth of an aging but rich divorcée.

"Your friend can wait for us here," Monzon said. He studied François, frowning, as to measure his tastes, then offered him a copy of *Time*. "We will go to my office."

Nothing in the office to suggest a dentist or even a busy man. A life-size bronze of a Rodin *Balzac* hovered in a corner, illuminated like a saint in a niche. On one wall a sepia mural photograph of the seafront façade of the Malecón in Havana. Langlade sank deeper than he wanted into his chair, the dentist stretched out on a recliner.

Monzon wanted to speak English, as though this would further protect their conversation from the absent François. He assured Langlade they were not being taped.

"My first point is that I don't want to know where he is. Don't tell me. And of course there must be nothing in writing anywhere."

"Quite, Carlos. I feel the same way. François will be our contact."

"I am surprised to see you into an affair of this order."

"I am not into it. I am a journalist, I intend to get a good story, nothing else, not a franc."

"Of course, Georges." Monzon smiled, the palms turned up appealingly, an actor on a small stage. "We want to do what is best for everybody concerned? Right? For democracy and progress. And best for the American too. He must be safely restored to his anxious colleagues."

"No one is anxious yet." Langlade looked at his watch. Not yet midnight. "They won't know anything for another seven or eight hours."

"During which he must be got to a safer place. You say a Sex Shop? Why on earth there?"

"Over the Sex Shop. It's where the taxi driver lives. So who would want our Assistant Secretary?"

"Who wouldn't want him? Forget for the moment the PLO and Libya and Iran. Think only of the Latinos who will be here in Paris. You know the list of the ten most wanted in the U.S. post offices? Any Assistant Secretary of State would be ipso facto on any list of the ten most hated in every country south of the Rio Grande. Hated by all the guerillas, of course. Salvador and Guatemala and Honduras. But resented by the governments too. And all need cash, governments and guerillas alike. Cash or ruin! Think only of Honduras. Do you know how much those wretched peasants got for their international banker. Ten million dollars. That put them on their feet for a while. Ten million dollars is enough to finance a rebellion of colonels. Or to destroy the rebellion."

"Randall is not an international banker," Langlade said. "The U.S. government is not going to pay ransom."

"There are patriots who would pay. Houston millionaires. Even old ladies among my patients who dream of returning to Havana and think the Randalls will get them there. I have only to stop drilling for a moment and the harangues begin. However, I do not want this to touch my practice in any way. You and I are strictly intermediaries working on behalf of a just solution. Right? We must not become principals."

"So who do you see as principals? Your Cuban friends in Miami?"

The reclining dentist fiddled with the controls of the recliner, and slowly rose to an upright position. He thus towered over Langlade.

"I will give you my thoughts, please do not interrupt.

Anything I do is for the sake of democracy and traditional values, that must be quite understood. First I ask who will pay a reasonable sum, say five million, to take over the responsibility of assuring Mr. Randall's safe return? The money to be spent in a good cause. Intermediaries who in turn will extract from Washington not money but reasonable concessions? Yes, I know. Washington has a policy of no concessions and no ransom money. Of course. Who doesn't say that? But suppose Washington used its influence to get a Colombian millionaire out of prison in return for Mr. Randall. Wouldn't that be worth five million to the Colombian's friends? Roque Amador, for instance. Wouldn't he pay that to have Randall in his hands? The first question is always this: *Who needs money and will be happy to sell Randall to the highest bidder?* The second question: *Who has money?* Who will spend five million for two good causes, first the release of a prisoner or two, second the release of Mr. Randall?"

"Who has money, Carlos? You."

"I'm too tired for joking."

"Let's say your friends in Miami."

"All right, yes, my friends in Miami. Wouldn't they put Mr. Randall to good use if they had him in their hands! Demand that Washington live up to its promises. Think of the last unrepentant Contras growing old in swamps! We are at the mercy of Washington's whims. It would indeed be nice to see Randall twist and turn."

"Rot for a while? Not released immediately? A year or two on bread and water?

"Don't look at me. I have nothing to do with it."

"Very well, your friends."

"They would hope to get more cooperation from the State Department. It's all very well to make speeches about human rights abuses in Cuba. I want my family's sugar mill back.

However, Miami and Havana are far away. Randall is in Paris and I also am in Paris. I don't want anyone breathing down my neck. I must not be involved."

"With your immense acquaintance..."

"Give me time to think," Monzon said.

"Time? We can't go beyond nine o'clock. By then the security people will insist on getting through to his room. It will be known he didn't sleep in his bed."

"The femme de chambre who got Randall into this mess?"

"She has the day off."

"She will have a good many days off. They must all three be removed to a reasonable and safe place: Randall, the femme de chambre, the taxi driver. Yes, and your friend the sportswriter. We do not want them around to make statements and misrepresent our role in this affair. You agree? There must be no independant excursions. They must be kept out of the way while we discover what good hands to put Randall into."

"François is all right. No point in tying him up."

"I don't like his looks," Monzon said. "Not at all. Already he knows too much."

The Sex Shop

The Assistant Secretary, who had dozed off, woke to the sound of Gabrielle crying. She was sitting opposite him in a straight chair, as though contemplating some move. Only ten minutes had elapsed. Luc had not returned.

For a moment Randall was so disoriented that he forgot he had been kidnapped. A pretty woman was crying, he was moved to console her.

"What's the matter?"

"I am ruined. The hotel will dismiss me. All because I wanted to help you. You seemed so sad, monsieur, so lonely! And I will tell you in all sincerity that I thought it would be nice to have an American friend. With the inflation it is necessary for a young girl without parents to do something. I could be your friend whenever you come to Paris. What are your affairs, monsieur? You are the chief of a great industry?"

"Just a tourist."

She wept again.

"Now because of Luc it will be impossible, our friendship. You will not forgive. You are the victim of Luc, I also am a victim. I had no idea he would play games." She moved toward him without getting up. Little hops forward of the straight chair until she was almost within reach. "I would be happy if we were back in your room in the Hotel Meurice. I would be content to begin it again, our relationship. I would say to you, *'That would be impossible, monsieur, to let you out the service entrance. But I would be happy to meet you somewhere for a little snack and to tell you about the interesting spectacles in Paris. The museums, for instance.'* That is what I should have said."

"It's not too late. Let me out now and we'll agree nothing has happened. Where's the key?"

"Luc has locked us up. Now you understand that I am not to blame, no?" The soulful brown eyes became crafty, long lines of thought appeared on her forehead. "Can I take the risk of resisting Luc? Why don't you, monsieur, telephone your friends at the hotel? Tell them where you are. They will come to get you."

The Assistant Secretary had not yet faced squarely the prospect of humiliating explanations, some of which might well reach Washington very quickly. It was all unthinkable, it was simply not happening. In another hour he would be back in his Meurice room. But to be taken in by a femme de chambre!

"Where are we? What is the address of the Bon Accueil?"

"If we are to act, we must act quickly. But not without reflection, monsieur. Obviously I must have some reward for the great risk I take in resisting Luc."

"Luc took all my money. You know that."

"I am an inexperienced poor girl from the provinces. Without parents. You are a rich man of affairs. What do you suggest?"

He got up, made a tentative move toward the telephone on the wall of the alcove. What was the French equivalent of 911?

"What's the name of the Sex Shop?"

"It has no other name, monsieur. In Paris there are hundreds of establishments, all called Sex Shop. Fifty, anyway."

"And probably fifty Bon Accueils. No?"

"At least. Listen to me, monsieur. There is nothing we can do now, for the moment. We will have to wait for Luc. But when Luc returns, then I will persuade him to call your American friends. They will pay Luc for the trouble he has had. As for me, I ask for nothing. Only to keep my job at the Hotel Meurice. Then we can begin again, you and I. Tomorrow we can meet for dinner, no? It is my day off. I know the best restaurants."

The Assistant Secretary was furious. But what could he say? He was also mesmerized by her expression of hurt innocence.

"I think not," he said. "But I won't say anything to the hotel. Not if you manage to get me out."

Gabrielle studied him. The lines of thought returned, making her look much older.

"I don't think you like my type, monsieur. You Americans prefer the fat Germans. Well, I have friends who are fat Nordic types. Big blue eyes, thick legs, splendid *poitrine*. I will be happy to introduce you."

"I like your type," he said. "That's not the problem."

Luc returned. He was carrying a net filet with pieces of a roasted chicken wrapped in newspaper, also a bottle which had been uncorked. Probably he had already taken a swig.

The label of the bottle said *Sancerre*.

"That is the wine of Hemingway," Randall said. Why on earth had he said that? The name would mean nothing to them.

"You appreciate the best French wine?" Luc said. He got a glass from the alcove and poured carefully. "Taste that! But no, you must drink at the same time that you eat the chicken. The wine is better with food."

He opened the grease-stained package and took out the chicken, which had been divided into four pieces. He handed Randall a thigh, forcefully.

"Give me a taste of the Sancerre," Gabrielle said.

Luc struck at the hand reaching for the bottle.

"Shut up and wait until I offer it to you. The American is our guest. He drinks first."

The chicken was still warm. The thigh with its crisp skin slid between his fingers. He caught it before it reached the floor.

"I'm not hungry."

"Eat while you can," Luc said in a friendly yet firm way. "We may have a long wait without food or anything to drink. Drink the good wine. First a taste of chicken, then the wine."

The Sancerre did not taste like Sancerre, but more like a fortified vin ordinaire. Or perhaps a bitter Gros Plant from the region of Nantes. Randall had, at his wife's prodding, acquired a knowledge of French wines. On several birthdays, also at Christmas, his wife gave him fat books on wine and haute cuisine.

"This is more like a Gros Plant," he said.

The words came with some difficulty, as though cotton, but a cotton soaked in alcohol, lined the roof of his mouth. His tongue felt very thick.

"Monsieur knows his wines," Gabrielle said, her voice coming as from far away.

"That is evident," Luc said, laughing. His laugh trailed off in an arpeggio of tinkling sounds, as though disappearing down a corridor.

The Assistant Secretary lay down and slept.

And yet he was, it seemed to him, sleeping with his eyes open, as though he couldn't summon even the strength to close them. The faces of Gabrielle and Luc floated above him in watery space, approaching and receding, friendly faces, though apparently detached from their bodies, faces showing a concern for his welfare. Yet their bodies existed, since first one, then both were taking his pulse. The fingers of Luc on his left wrist were rough, the fingers of a workman, whereas those of Gabrielle were smooth. Her soft silky fingertips probed for the vein so invitingly that the vein responded, the awakened blood apparently rising until, he surmised, the vein was swollen twice its normal size. But there were always precautions to be taken, the friendliness might go away, the nails might dig in. He tried to move his hands, to rid himself of their pulse-taking, or at least to rid himself of Luc's. But his wrists and hands could not move. They were held down as by strong cold hands, Luc's hands, a hand on each wrist. The soft fingers of Gabrielle were gone. He closed his eyes.

Or had he? In the immobility of his limbs he seemed to

be awake in this dingy room in Paris, Luc's room, a room above a Sex Shop. Yet he was also in a spotless doctor's office, on Connecticut Avenue to be exact, and about to receive a precautionary injection on the eve of his long deferred journey to Central America. There he would be tested, to begin with in El Salvador, on all he had learned from the many briefings by underlings, academics with no knowledge of real life. Tested too on what he had picked up in two weeks of "total immersion" in the Spanish language, lessons from a nervous Honduran refugee who aspired to a green card. Everyone down there would speak English, yet it would surely be helpful to sprinkle a few choice comments in their own language, a word of flattery, it might be, for a president's wife.

The doctor who was injecting him at this very moment was himself probably Hispanic, and would appreciate a few Spanish words. But he felt too tired to speak. The few words would have to wait.

And now, surely, he dreamed, although less blissfully than before. He was bored and restless in his room high above the few lights of the ruined city, no lights at all where the buildings had not been reconstructed. He was bored, yes. And so longed to descend into the city, anonymously of course, even to venture into the stinking dark streets away from the Avenida. All all hateful. Hateful the President's wife with her jeweled fat and her chatter about the native poet, hateful her hand on his wrist, the hand sweaty yet firmly holding him as she assured him of the President's esteem, even though at this moment the oily President was addressing someone across the table in a Spanish of the gutter. How would he know it as Spanish of the gutter had he not, in his seldom recognized love of democracy, wandered more than once in those stinking streets, stepping carefully over the open sewers and the naked infants sprawling in the doorways? Hateful the murmuring voices in the dark huts sunk in their garlic odors of charcoal and excrement, the mumbled slogans, the hitched-up trousers and macho ravings of the urban guerillas, the wretched committees typing lists of abuses by candlelight or writing them by hand. When had the receptionist last had a bath?

And yet he had loved it, the heat and the chattering bronze shopgirls, and the dark descent into the street, in pursuit for instance of the plump waitress Dolores who, after putting the check on his table, had nimbly slipped a folded note under his curved fingers, so nimbly that she must have done it more than once before, even at the risk of losing her job. The fingers under his hand were hot, her hip also was hot as it somehow contrived to touch his wrist, so hot in fact as to seem flesh rather than cloth. *I like you American boy take me to nightclub please 10 P.M. O.K.* He laughed out loud, but in a friendly way, at the preposterous notion of himself, the envoy whose mere presence in the city could mean millions, in weapons if not cash, accompanying a plump hotel waitress to a nightclub where, it might well be, he would encounter the President himself with one or another of his girlfriends. Would they be asked to join the President's party? He nevertheless left a sufficiently large tip, in itself a clear message, and he was waiting in a taxi when the waitress emerged from the restaurant at ten o'clock, and to his surprise headed at once for his taxi. He had the odd impression that all this had happened before, possibly in Managua if not Guatemala, then it was a waitress named Lourdes, the taxi coughing as though it would never start, instructed by the doorman to take him to the Embassy but diverted instead to the edge of the slum beyond which it was impossible for the taxi to go. He followed her on foot and at last into a candlelit hut swarming with infants, not to mention an old crone smoking a cigar. On that evening the waitress Lourdes eluded him. So too, in Managua or was it Salvador, the waitress Dolores eluded him.

But not forever, since he accepted her invitation to accompany her to the beach of hot sand and fierce sun, where she at once lay down and invited him to lie beside her. Vendors approached with tortillas, also starving dogs. Without delay, nevertheless, with only a few words of obscure endearment, she had begun to fumble at his trousers, even though several children were standing a few feet away, watching. She indicated with firmness that his trousers were to be removed, the shorts also. She examined the shorts with amusement, feeling the cloth and muttering comments. He tried to resist her manipulations, the hand that already enclosed his awakening penis, the shorts now quite gone and his flesh responding to the fierce sun even more than to the descending mouth. The mouth that enclosed him had, oddly, the texture of sand, warm moist sand, but living sand, sand that rythmically pulsed and writhed. It was the writhing of a coiling and uncoiling serpent, now threatening to uncoil fatally. He held his breath. Could it be possible that he was about to spend himself in sand? It was important to withdraw before it was too late.

The children were still watching. But behind them stood a man with a camera, very possibly a native journalist. The journalist was clicking away even as he, the Assistant Secretary, tore himself free from both mouth and sand.

All this had happened before.

Or had it? It was Luc who was standing above him with the camera. The girl Gabrielle, who was wearing a mask, was in other respects naked. So too was the Assistant Secretary. He was astonished to find that he was bound to the bed. And not by ropes but by chains!

"He made me do it," Gabrielle said. "You are a victim, monsieur. I also am a victim."

monday

The Photographs

THREE-THIRTY OF A WET PARIS morning, but sensuously warm in the office of Dr. Carlos Monzon as he studied the pictures spread on his desk. He was seated and at ease in his Balzacian robe while Langlade had to stand at his elbow if he was to have a close look. Still at least four hours of grace before Randall's absence would be discovered. Since their earlier meeting Langlade had enriched his knowledge of the Assistant Secretary from the files and data base of the *Herald* and the *Express*. Randall, in his official capacity, was not much admired, in France.

Two small statues of polished marble adorned the desk, one a bust of Napoleon, the other a shy *Psyche*, with one hand sheltering the breasts, another the mons veneris. Also a box of cigars. The statue of Psyche was faintly smudged, as though the dentist liked to fondle it when lost in thought.

He rearranged the photographs.

"Does the fool Luc keep chains in his room?"

"The chains without doubt came from the Sex Shop. Only Sex Shops sell chains like that, and not every Sex Shop."

"Which means the flics will take only an hour or so to find the Sex Shop in question, and be directed upstairs to the driver's apartment. Right? So the driver is already doomed, ten years if he is lucky, the Meurice slut also, although the mask gives her some protection. Any tattoos on her body?"

"Don't see any."

Monzon took a silver rimmed magnifying glass from his desk and ran it carefully over the best of the prints, examining first Randall, dwelling for a moment on the loins. Was there not a very small chain there too? The mask left the girl truly anonymous, the more so because her wide open mouth, engulfing the Assistant Secretary's penis, distorted the rest of her features. Thomas Randall, however, was wearing no mask. His hands were curved in sensual ease, in spite of the manacled wrists and ankles. His eyes were closed. But it was still possible to detect a faint beatific smile. An unbiased observer would conclude that his chained presence on the bed was entirely voluntary, and that he had probably paid a considerable sum to satisfy his peculiar though far from unique tastes.

"The smile should add fifty thousand to the value of the pictures," Monzon said. He directed his attention to the masked Gabrielle and ran his glass over her curved legs and graceful back. "They must be moved. The girl must be kept with Randall. She must remain in responsible hands, even if he is released."

"So she can't talk? Why not as your new receptionist?"

The dentist ignored this impertinence and continued to study Gabrielle. He reached for a cigar without moving the magnifying glass.

"How rich is he?"

"Just moderately. His father was a lawyer who spent a lot of time defending leftists pro bono. For the love of humanity, if not to appease his conscience. He died when the boy was very young, couldn't have left very much. Did you know Randall was one of the crazy radicals himself? He was even arrested with a mob of other students in one of the big university protests of those days. No, I don't think he's rich enough to pay for the photographs. Nothing all that extraordinary in the assets, even though his wife is a lot richer than he."

"How rich?"

Langlade shrugged.

"Don't know. Randall went to the University of California, then the Georgetown Law School in Washington. Yes, he was one of the crazies. But he must have changed after he got into the government. One of the stories in *Time* suggests this happened after his first trip to Central America. It was one of those commissions sent down to find out what it already knows, has already decided. Something happened down there that turned him around. He acquired a firmer understanding of the communist menace. That probably got him his real promotion. But money? My guess Randall really doesn't care too much about money. It's only a guess."

"I care about money," Monzon said. "What do you suggest?"

Langlade pondered the question. The problem, in a nutshell, was to know who would pay a reasonable sum—say two million, which might launder down to one—for the physical possession of Randall. Whoever paid the two million could then make larger demands in the interest of politics or ideology or, simply, the State Department's good name. Five million, say, either that or adequate political concessions. His own modest reward to come from the story and first publication of the pictures. The story for one of the great weeklies, a second story for the *Express,* the pictures to go to one of the monthlies devoted to erotic confessions or revelations.

"Let me remind you I don't want any money," Langlade said.

"Don't be silly," Monzon said.

"Just the story."

"Who would you try to sell it to first? *Stern*? Obviously there are two separate operations to consider: number one, the pictures, number two, Randall's person. Or vice-versa. Let's predicate first the release of the Assistant Secretary to be paid for, then the pictures. And sufficient assurance that no more pictures exist. The word of a man they can trust. Yourself, for instance. So we are talking of two levels of payment. No?"

"The pictures must be published. They have historical importance. A serious journalist has certain obligations to the public—"

"But published only after they have been used for leverage."

"The government won't pay a cent," Langlade said. "So they will announce at once. But disgrace is disgrace. The clean State Department image of competence, its high moral mission. And Randall has his little secrets. He must know everything an Assistant Secretary needs to know about the

CIA in Central America. Of course. So I think the government could well make concessions. Reasonable but secret concessions."

"Someone must pay cash for the opportunity to demand concessions from Washington? Is that it?"

"Don't ask me questions, Carlos. I am only a serious journalist reporting a story of historical interest." He picked up one of the photographs and examined it from several angles. "Think of what Cuba could do with these pictures. Would Fidelito try to get rid of a trade barrier?"

"He's not that much of a fool. I think he would just want to humiliate. Humiliate Randall, humiliate the State Department. Maybe he would invite writers or movie people and a few congressmen down for a cultural conference and suddenly flash Randall and the girl on the screen. Right in the middle of a film on Cuban ballet. Or just pass the pictures around surreptitiously and wait for the media to take care of them. Slightly doctored pictures so as not to offend the TV audience. However, Cuba doesn't have that kind of money."

"So the money has to come from your side, Carlos? From your rich friends in Miami? Some of them will be in Paris for the conference. As 'observers'."

Monzon laughed. It was more like a cough.

"I am invited to the reception. Not to the conference, to the reception at the Lutétia."

"So am I."

"My rich friends. Yes, I can well imagine someone—not a committee, more likely an individual—paying a million for the pleasure of personally releasing the pictures to the press. All the more satisfaction if he did it after Randall had been ransomed."

Langlade was becoming impatient.

"Don't use words like 'ransomed'. Aren't there any serious men among your friends? Wouldn't they try for some real change of policy?"

"Unfortunately you can't use a hostage to effect a change of policy. The hostage gets home safe and the new policy is revoked. What concessions could they get out of the administration that Congress wouldn't cut off?"

"You are being very negative, Carlos."

"There are still the rich widows, the fanatics, the evangelists, the sultans, the World Anti-Communist League. I think they could be induced to pay for Randall's release and perhaps also for the pictures for the good name of the cause. However, we are not in Houston or Dallas or Los Angeles. We are in France."

"How about the Haitians in France? They too feel they have been betrayed. Why couldn't Washington have allowed them to have their penthouse in New York?"

"Baby Doc's millions? It's an idea. Yes, a nice idea. I have my connections there, Hypollite Jasmin, a patient with the worst teeth I have ever treated. But for the moment our problem is to get Randall and his companions out of the Sex Shop and to a safe place. What do you think of the catacombs?"

"The catacombs where the French Resistance had their hidden headquarters? Under Denfert Rochereau? You're joking, Carlos. Tourists go through all the time."

"Not those catacombs. Smaller ones, quite off the tourist track. You remember Rolando Santander? At the moment he's involved with some Basque separatists, right here in Paris. And there are other possibilities."

Monzon began to play with the buttons on his desk. The room lights went out, although the statue of Balzac in his niche still glowed. A panel on the wall moved to reveal a large plastic map of Paris with many small glass dots. By touching further buttons he could change the dots to red or green lights. The map existed for the dentist's late hours of solitary relaxation. He was a student of history, and enjoyed replaying turbulent moments of the Paris past. Street by street he could follow the retreat of the communards to their last stand in Père Lachaise.

"Look!"

He rapidly extinguished the lights until only two remained, one near St. Lazare, one in the far reaches of the fifteenth arrondissement.

"Somewhere near here is your Sex Shop. And here are my 'catacombs'. Small catacombs."

The game of disappearing lights made the journalist uneasy.

"Remember I'm only an observer," he said. "I don't want any of the money."

El Tigre

There must have been further sips of Sancerre, even another injection by the Hispanic doctor, since he slept again.

The Assistant Secretary had found it hard to take his plight seriously until this second awakening, this time on the stone floor of a room without windows and whose walls were also of stone. Even the ultimate humiliation of the photographs could presumably be taken care of by money. But now, shivering with cold and with his back aching and his wrists and ankles still sore where the chains had been, it occurred to him that he might not be present at this afternoon's reception or at the head of the conference table the next morning. His watch was gone, but he assumed he had awakened to another day. If his kidnappers found out who he was his plight would indeed be serious, more serious than he wanted to contemplate. Whatever happened, he must not reveal his identity.

Sitting up, he discovered that his own clothes were gone. He was wearing the baggy blue trousers and rough smock of a Paris workman, a truck driver or stevedore. Even his fine shirt of Egyptian cotton was gone. The coarse denim scraped his skin. The Assistant Secretary thought of himself as a man of strength and ardor. Yet the loss of his clothes, together with the memory of the chains, left him with a strange sense of deprivation, even of sadness, as though his very willpower, that anchor of political and personal strength, had begun to dissolve.

From the next room came the strident voices of men speaking very rapidly in Spanish, all of them speaking at once. The FMLN had sent an observer to the conference, so too Guatemalan guerillas, though of course they were not invited. Would they, if they captured him, dare put pressure on the American delegation by holding him for a few hours? Was it possible Luc and Gabrielle were not lying, and a limousine with terrorists unknown to them had followed their taxi from the Meurice? No, he did not think it was possible.

Nevertheless these were Spanish voices, now joined by the voice of a woman speaking in French. It sounded like Gabrielle.

A door opened: it was Gabrielle. She was carrying a tray on which was a large mug, also half a baguette. She smiled briskly and gave him a little curtsey, precisely as though she were entering his room in the Meurice, with himself propped up in bed under the reclining rosy Boucher. She put the tray on the stone floor beside him, a very milky *café au lait*.

She knelt in front of him, still smiling. Her brown eyes were without malice.

"You are cute like that, in your worker's smock." So she dared to *tutoyer* him! *Tu es mignon comme ça, dans ton costume d'ouvrier.* She ran her hand over the rough cloth of his smock. She was wearing a flowered summer dress with a deep V-neck. Her perfume was rich and smoky. Under her gaze his indignation hung in abeyance. He was fascinated by her skilled acting, as though it had no relation to his "real life." The Molière soubrette, he himself the country bumpkin.

He was enraged. His hand trembled, the mug of coffee fell to the floor. Falling, the coffee soaked her bright skirt. She stepped back, her brown eyes shocked, then filling with tears.

"I'm sorry. Please get me another cup of coffee, this time black."

"This is what the brutes gave me. In the Hotel Meurice there would be flowers in cut glass, orange juice on ice, croissants and brioches, several confitures. However, that might cost you a hundred and fifty francs. More, if you demanded eggs. Here the breakfast is free."

"The brutes?"

"You are a prisoner. Me also. We are prisoners of Spanish men, Basque terrorists I think. As for Luc, I don't know what happened to him."

She left with the mug of coffee and was back minutes later.

"Drink your coffee. Eat the bread, even though it is horrible. It is important to keep up the morale. The nourishment gives strength."

"What kind of idiot do you take me for? I know you arranged everything. Just tell me how much you want and I'll tell you how to get it. And stop lying."

"You permit?" She took a sip from his coffee and broke

off a piece of the bread. "It is you who lie, monsieur. Why did you tell me your name was 'Iss'? I thought you were a big business man, not a high functionary of the United States. And now perhaps I am truly ruined. I would not have dreamed of taking a high functionary down the back elevator and out the *sortie de service*. What should I call you? Monsieur le ministre, perhaps?"

"Who saw the pictures?"

"I don't know anything about it. Imagine! What if my boyfriend saw the pictures of me doing that."

"I thought Luc was your boyfriend."

"Luc is only a pal. I ask myself what happened to him." The brown eyes again filled with tears. "My reputation in France as a serious young woman is finished. You are furious, monsieur, with good reason. But I too am furious. Why didn't you say you were an important functionary? A man who might be kidnapped by terrorists."

"Who told you who I was?"

"The Spanish types who brought us here. Soon they will let us go I hope, but still I am ruined. What will I do? With your influence you can get me a job in a hotel in Washington. I think they like French femmes de chambre there, no? Which is the best hotel?"

He almost laughed. In another life he would have wanted to embrace her. What had happened to his rage?

"The Willard might be about right for you," he said. "You can roll some more functionaries there."

Their conversation was interrupted by a man wearing a mask. He motioned for Randall to follow him to the room's second door. Could it be Luc? When Gabrielle offered to come too he waved her off.

"You wait here!" he said with a decidedly Hispanic accent. No, it was not Luc.

This second room also had a floor and walls of stone. There was a large carpet, probably Moroccan, and many framed photographs on the wall. A desk with no papers or telephone. A plain straight chair stood alone in the very center of the room. Was the straight chair for him or for his interrogator? It was still to be assumed, hoped indeed, that his questioner would be the taxi driver Luc, though it was obvious that others had become involved.

Waiting, he inspected the wall photographs, which appeared to commemorate the events of a lifetime, with inscriptions in white ink. The same face appeared in all of them, at first youthful, smiling and optimistic, with no trace of beard, but later worn and bearded and with a slashed scar running from the left ear to the corner of a white moustache. The Assistant Secretary knew that face. Rolando Santander, known through more than forty years of shifting loyalties as El Tigre. Two years ago he had disappeared from Miami after a meeting of the diehard Contra remnant. It was assumed he had been terminated at that time. It was now apparent that assumption was wrong.

Would such a man not appreciate the department's undeviating support of those who respect order, authority and progress? Surely he would listen to reason.

One of the earliest pictures (with the caption *Cayo Confites*) showed him arm and arm with a jovial young Fidel Castro, the two men stripped to the waist. Behind them a ragtag band of soldiers lounging on a sandy beach. It was an expedition intended to overthrow "The Benefactor" Trujillo that was aborted by the State Department. Even Santander was a dreamer in those days, with fantasies of Caribbean liberation. In an adjoining photograph, now dressed as a cowboy and with a long horsewhip coiled over his arm, he stood beside the Benefactor himself, splendid in medals and

ribbons. It was the first of many photographs to show Santander with a whip. In one, now years older and with a
pointed black beard, he was poised to whip a prisoner whose
back showed many scars. *Costanza,* nine years later. Behind
the prisoner were a number of smiling men in business suits
and ties. Still in the Dominican Republic, Randall surmised,
although a general sitting in an armchair at the far right of
the picture might have been one of the Somozas. How con-
fusing it all was, to have so many Trujillos and Somozas!
Years older, and now in immaculate white guayabera, white
trousers and shoes, Santander appeared in a nightclub act,
but a very private nightclub. The end of the long whip, surely
twenty feet long, had just coiled itself about the naked torso
of a woman dancer. The next picture indicated that she
danced toward him, rolling herself in the whip, which extended from waist to bare breasts. In a third she had danced
away from the whip, unrolling herself, with a long welt
showing across the back.

The Assistant Secretary studied the photographs with
mounting discomfort. In a blurred, less professional picture,
a much older Santander was shown with the whip over his
left arm while the extended right hand held a pistol at the
head of a kneeling prisoner. He was wearing the uniform of
a National Guardsman. *Muerto del porco communista 1981.* He
was still older in a group picture of Contra guerillas, the slash
from ear to moustache now present, and the small beard
quite white. *Morazon, 1984.* How long was it after this that
Santander, after quarreling with the leaders in Miami, disappeared? Had he survived, then, that Miami liquidation?
Or was the gallery of photographs created by a nostalgic
Paris disciple?

He had indeed survived, since another door opened and
the aged Santander appeared in a wheelchair that he rapidly

propelled toward the Assistant Secretary. Across his lap was a tartan robe tucked in as by loving hands, and on the robe was a coiled whip. His shirt was open over a massive chest entirely covered with curling white hairs. The white beard was stained and matted, the long scar was corrugated and a sandy gray.

So the single straight chair was for himself. Santander pointed to it commandingly.

"Take off your shirt!"

The voice was anything but feeble. It resonated as from deep in a vault. Automatically the Assistant Secretary reached for buttons, but the workman's smock had none. And to pull the shirt over his head was too humiliating. The coiled whip, on the other hand, had metallic studs. The whip even seemed to be stirring with life, though still coiled on the invalid's lap.

The Assistant Secretary decided it would be wise to temporize, even flatter.

"I was fascinated by the pictures, Mr. Santander. You have had a long and interesting history. All the way back to Cayo Confites."

"So you know who I am? So much the worse for you." The whip rose from his lap as from its own volition, but now a hairy hand was stroking it. "I repeat: Take off your shirt. Turn around and kneel. For the moment I am concerned only with your back."

To take off the shirt might be a reasonable precaution, even to turn the back could protect more vulnerable parts. But he was determined not to kneel.

"You are making a terrible mistake. We have the best high-tech communications. Everyone knows that. The Embassy will already know where I am."

But he was protesting in vain. The whip had already been raised.

Pariscope

When by nine o'clock Randall had still not called for his breakfast, or made other sign of life, and with his phone still obstinately blocked, the three most concerned agreed it was time to go to his room: the American escort Bush, the French special agent Le Moal, the hotel security man Chameau. There they found the bed neatly turned down but obviously not slept in. No sign of disorder in bathroom, dressing room, or Louis XVI salon other than a discarded banana peel beside the basket of fruit and unopened bottle of champagne. There were, however, papers on the marquetry desk in the salon: an airline ticket folder, a number of pencilled notes on a sheet of hotel stationery, the thin red Michelin guide of Paris restaurants and hotels, and PARISCOPE, a guide to entertainments. It was open to a page that included PEEP-SHOW, MIMODRAME, THEATRE LOVING-CHAIR, as well as LES TELEPHONES DES PLAISIRS. Under this last heading, *Délirophone*, *Hot-Line* and *Les Tigresses* were all willing to accept checks and credit cards.

"All that is disquieting," Le Moal said. "Put a little toe in that mud, soon one is engulfed."

"If it were only the toe," the Meurice security man said, smiling sadly. "I have faced this problem before."

"Still, some of these establishments are correct. I believe our distinguished visitor has had an amusing night, perhaps with one of the tigresses. He may turn up any minute." He pointed a long finger at the American escort Bush. "Too bad you did not accompany him. You might have found it amusing.''

The notes, evidently for the first meeting, read:

> *Commie threat persists: quote Fitzpatrick*
> *Guerillas implacable*
> *The Che Guevara heritage*
> *Trade not aid*
> *Elections fraudulent*
> *The six freedoms (don't talk too fast).*

None of the call girl services had been marked by the Assistant Secretary. There was, however, a restaurant circled near the end of the Michelin guide, in the working class nineteenth arrondissement, perhaps the last part of Paris an American diplomat would be likely to go, unless to one of the famous steak places on the Avenue Jean Jaurès. But the modest restaurant he had marked was far from the Avenue Jean Jaurès.

La Chaumière, 46 avenue Secretan. 42 06 54 89.

''An excellent little place of its class,'' the police officer Le Moal commented. ''A commendable *ris de veau*. But there is only one reason a distinguished diplomat would dine there.''

''To meet someone in confidence?''

''Of course. We will have a man down there at once. A few questions.''

The more embarrassing problem remained. How did the Assistant Secretary get out of the hotel unseen? Could he have slipped out the rue de Rivoli entrance to buy an English book at Galignani a few doors down?

''Out of the question,'' Chameau said. ''And the rue de

Castiglione door is always locked, except for the grand receptions."

"The entrance for the personnel?"

"Most unlikely. The guard is always there in his box. He would know if an outsider tried to get by. Moreover, he would have been seen by the doorman at the porte-cochère. That's only a few meters down the street."

"True. But the doorman might have been at his telephone."

Reluctantly the three men reported their findings to their superiors and awaited their reprimands. In the Embassy a first crisis meeting was held shortly after ten: the Ambassador, still unshaven, the chief security officer Chalmers, the CIA station chief Trent, who was listed in the directory under a different title, something to do with economic affairs. They were joined a few minutes later by the press attaché Winton Miles, whose career might hang on keeping such incidents quiet.

It was to be assumed the insufferable Randall (*"insupportable,"* the Ambassador said, proud of his improving French) would turn up shortly after his night's debauch. Notifying Washington could be held off until noon here, six in the morning there. But if Randall was still absent at noon the Costa Rican vice-chairman of the conference on Latin America would have to be notified. The Assistant Secretary had experienced a disagreeable gastrointestinal episode with a light fever. He was being treated at the Embassy and would stay there in seclusion. His presence at this afternoon's reception was problematical.

"The French will be itching to get a search underway," the station chief said. "The DST and DGSE will be here any minute, I imagine. Not to mention Police Action. Maybe even the GN."

"What's the GN?" the Ambassador asked.

"Gendarmerie Nationale."

"I thought they were only in the country."

"In theory, yes. But in France nobody wants to be left out."

The Ambassador turned to his press attaché.

"I'm counting on you to keep this out of the French press. Only the traveler's sickness, not a word more. A one-sentence handout. Do you have any idea what the disappearance of an Assistant Secretary of State would mean here, not to mention at home?" He tried another French word, slowly. "The *retentissement*."

"I certainly do. But there will be no little reaction if we try to cover up."

"I didn't *say* 'cover up.' "

They would wait until noon. A few minutes before noon, however, an incident occurred in the room adjoining the press attaché's office, where three secretaries had gathered for a long-planned luncheon. They were sharing an aperitif, inexpensive because purchased from the Embassy commissary, before going down to the cafeteria. The FAX machine had quietly produced a document.

"What next?" the press attaché's own secretary said. "I think I'll just let it lay there. It can wait."

One of the other secretaries gave the document an idle glance. She screamed: a good-natured, amused scream.

"I can't *believe* it!"

What had emerged was the slightly blurred photograph of a naked man whose outstretched wrists and ankles were chained, the four metal bands being attached to a pole that extended the length of his recumbent body. He was lying on a bed. A masked woman, a frivolous metal-studded mask covering the eyes to give the impression of a cat, was bent over the man's loins and had his penis in her mouth. The man was smiling. His eyes were closed.

On the bed beside them, as though waiting to be used, was a complicated metallic instrument attached to a studded belt. A circular opening beneath the belt could perhaps be used for the penis. From it a weight hung, the kind of weight still used in old-fashioned wall clocks, but smaller. Much smaller.

None of the secretaries recognized the man as Randall. They conferred.

"What a riot! But who on earth would put that through our FAX? I think I'll show it to Mr. Miles."

"I wouldn't. That other thing. Is that for fun or is it supposed to hurt?"

"Probably both."

All three laughed.

Their laughter attracted the press attaché, who had appeared at his door.

"What's the big joke?"

"Look what came over the FAX."

The press attaché, whose mind was on something else, stared at the sheet, put it down with a shrug. Somebody at the *Tribune* office, probably, having fun with the machine. He picked it up again, studied the blurred features of the Assistant Secretary. Only minutes before he had been told of the PARISCOPE on Randall's desk, open to the sex pages.

"Jesus Christ!"

Would the same machine disgorge within minutes a first notice that demands would presently be made? Or would they have to wait days or even weeks? This was the press attaché's first diplonapping experience. It would also be the Ambassador's first.

Heads would certainly roll.

He folded the FAX'd photograph and put it in his breast pocket. What the secretaries didn't know wouldn't hurt them.

"Some sick joke," he said. "Enjoy your lunch."

The Ambassador was informed of the FAX photo as he was about to go out to lunch. A second crisis meeting lasted only minutes. The Assistant Secretary had to be found, whatever the risk of a leak to the press. It was reluctantly decided that the French, who had jurisdiction over any criminal affair, would have to be told of the photo. An innocent dinner in a modest restaurant in an unfashionable part of Paris (but why there? who was he meeting? why didn't he have his bodyguard?) had evidently been followed by one of the enterprises offering the pleasures of bondage for pay. Expensive but not necessarily dangerous. He had not, however, returned. And now, given the FAX, the possibilities for blackmail and ransom were infinite. Washington and the French services had to know. No statements to the press.

It was the lunch hour, a sacred time, but the French machine rumbled into action. The Minister of the Defense was about to dine on *homard breton aux artichaux* at Grand Véfour, the Minister of the Interior was at Lasserre, and had ordered *blanc de turbot à la gelée d'oseille*, to be followed by *soufflé chaud au cacao et noix*. At the Quai d'Orsay the Minister of Foreign Affairs, again preoccupied with Lebanon, was having a simple snack at his desk: *noisettes d'agneau en chevreuil*. All three left the table earlier than they had planned. Gone were the heroic times of four-hour lunches at which the fate of a colony could be decided, or the administration of the Banque de France.

At the Elysée the President, still hard at work, paused only long enough to comment that it was no more than the Assistant Secretary deserved. For too long Randall and his superiors had seen evil motives in every pronouncement of the diminished but still puissant enemy. In a changed world they found it hard to put their paranoia aside. Now it would be Randall's turn to summon motives in explanation of a glaring imprudence. Tomorrow, perhaps even today, would come the déluge, with cautious statements to the press and a reasoned defense of French security practices. There were limits to what one could do to counteract a diplomat's folly! Meanwhile one could reflect with satisfaction that the intractable Randall's days were probably numbered. One could hope for a more moderate U.S. attitude and hence replacement.

Already the massive search operation was underway. "Round up the usual perverts!" the Prefect of Police ordered, when given a first censored description of the FAX'd photograph. Agents from the Direction de la Surveillance du Territoire (DST) studied the pertinent two pages of PARISCOPE (on which twenty-five different establishments were advertised), visited the Assistant Secretary's suite and interrogated all personnel of the Hotel Meurice and of the small nineteenth arrondissement restaurant La Chaumière. Two young Americans had dined there after visiting the famous tombs of Père Lachaise. No others. At exactly what hour had the Assistant Secretary, bent on suspect pleasures, slipped out of the hotel? Was he is his room when, around seven o'clock, the femme de chambre would have turned down his bed? Today was her day off. An agent would be sent to her address for questions. Meanwhile a team from the Renseignements et Action of the DGSE, although commissioned to protect external security, had begun a round of the Sex Shops. First the cluster near Pigalle to Clichy, then the thick constellation on the rue St. Denis, at last the rue de la Gaieté. No time for the isolated shops on back streets. The Renseignements Generaux itself, Section Violence Politique, was already at its computers, and even its dogeared *fiches*, pulling in troublemakers known for their anti-American sentiments.

By two o'clock the first journalists, noting so much activity in the French agencies, were on the trail. What was up? By four it was widely rumored, in spite of Embassy denials, that a FAX photo of a chained man resembling the Assistant Secretary had been received at the Embassy. *France-Soir* knew earlier than the rest, and was already on the streets with scare headlines. Two o'clock in Paris, eight o'clock in Washington. At the White House a skilled cartoonist, working from National Security's coded description of the photograph, had a version of Randall's plight ready for the President's eyes. A woman with her back to the viewer was leaning over the chained man tendentiously, but what she was actually doing was left to the imagination. A large question mark filled the space denoting the man's head. The President, however, had been informed of the chained man's beatific smile. It was the embarrassing smile that led him to shift the burden of crisis management from the White House to State.

"Let them look out after their own," he said quietly.

"And still deny?"

"Of course. There wasn't any photograph, so there's nothing to deny. Or else say it was a crude forgery."

A NEW MAN, GRAY-HAIRED and rather disheveled, joined the Embassy crisis task force for its third meeting of the day: the cultural attaché Gordon Seymour. A Francophile of long standing, and therefore suspect, he would nevertheless be representing the Embassy at the Hotel Lutètia reception for the conference delegates. He might, in the absence of the Assistant Secretary, sit in on the first meeting of the conference. He could even be helpful. He had written one book and a number of articles on French politics, even a long article that sorted out the myriad French intelligence services. No mean achievement. At least he knew all the acronyms, which was more than could be said for the CIA station chief. His life had to some extent been determined by his service in the OSS in the war. He had been parachuted into the maquis, joined the search for collaborators after the liberation, and for several years after the war remained in Paris with the USIS. His mild socialist sympathies made a career in State impossible, however, and he went into academia. He was the kind of man the extreme rightists of that time wanted to ruin. He became an expert on contemporary France, though by no means a famous one. Now, only a year short of retirement, he had been appointed to the agreeable post of cultural attaché. Perhaps the gift of a former student? He never found out. But anyone could tell at a glance that he was a professor. Shoes and shirt collar were worn, the lapels of his jacket were of an earlier era. His marriage had ended ten years before. Now he lived in a gloomy apartment on the rue Jacob. An Embassy secretary filled in when he was obliged to entertain.

He was pleasantly surprised to be brought into the loop, although his chair was placed at the far end of the table from the Ambassador. There were glasses of water for everyone, but only he was not given a note pad. His presence was in a sense unofficial.

The Embassy security officer Chalmers reported on the first Washington response. Already the White House had dumped this unfortunate affair onto State. Someone there had offered a first assessment of the kidnappers' possible motives:

1. The release of prisoners. Medellín Cartel? Iran? the PLO?
2. To get names of CIA agents in Latin America?
3. Money and publicity for guerrilla action?
4. Bargain release of frozen assets? Libya? Cuba?
5. Communist revenge against Randall the hard-liner?
6. A political statement on eve of the conference. To be released during conference?
7. Action Directe? Red Brigade? Basque separatists?
8. Amateurs?

The security officer went around the table asking for opinions. In Gordon Seymour's opinion it was the work of amateurs. Professionals would have withheld the FAX for a time. The Ambassador leaned to the theory of a political statement by leftist groups who were in Paris, hoping to influence the conference deliberations. A few would be at the Lutétia reception, also several Cuban and Nicaraguan exile dignitaries invited in a gesture of good will. Perhaps Randall would be released that very evening. But what would his captors do with the photograph? Somewhere in Paris a copy, perhaps several copies, existed in malicious hands. Those hands must be found. No one must see the Assistant Secretary's smiling acceptance of his bondage. Certainly not the French press.

The years dropped away as Gordon Seymour listened. The descent onto a field in the Cévennes lit only by automobile lights, the months of genial fraternity with the maquisards, the intoxications of the liberation, two exciting postwar missions for the OSS. His asthma, his arthritis, his gray hairs were momentarily forgotten.

The Embassy security officer was looking at him impatiently. His face must have revealed his daydreaming.

"Are you still with us, Gordon? There's a beanpole named Pierre Perdoux from the DGSE waiting. He has been sent over to work with us. I daresay it's so he can report on what we're doing. I don't want him poking around. Why don't you play along with him and keep him out of trouble? Take him over to the Meurice. Talk politics with him. Buy him a drink. Keep him busy." Chalmers smiled, an unpleasantly complacent smile. "Maybe you and he can find the kidnappers."

"I'm sure," Gordon said. "But I'm not to let him find the pornography?"

The Ambassador adjusted his glasses, scrutinized the worn shirt.

"I trust you'll be changing for the reception."

So that was how he found himself in the bedroom of the Meurice suite, in the presence of an exceptionally cool and elegant assistant manager in a dress worthy of Dior, and with the humiliating assignment of keeping the French agent Perdoux away from the Embassy. The agent was all of six feet two, appeared to be in his early thirties, and was almost bald. He had many teeth, sunken eyes, and a foolish smile. His sports jacket sagged. The assistant manager could not conceal her surprise on inspecting Gordon's card. A seedy cultural relations attaché in the company of an ugly young flic, inquiring into the scabrous behavior of a diplomat!

"You will pardon me if I show a bit of impatience. You are the fifth and sixth men this afternoon to ask to see the suite. There have been three from the French services, one from your Embassy. Will there be more?"

"I hope not," Gordon said.

"What an admirable decor," Perdoux said. "A splendid Fragonard, that, over the bed."

"Boucher, I believe. What can I possibly show you that has any rapport with your inquiry?"

Gordon decided to flatter her intelligence.

"What is your opinion, madame? How do you think Mr. Randall left the hotel without being seen?"

"I have no idea."

"The rue de Rivoli entrance to the restaurant?"

"It would be impossible. The maître d'hôtel would see him. Also the waiters."

"If a mouche were to take him out by the service entrance? Or the femme de chambre? The woman who turned down his bed?"

"Gabrielle? It would be against the rules. Only the personnel use that entrance. Moreover, the guard controls everyone who enters or leaves."

"But it would be possible? In principle?"

She shrugged, dismissed the idea of incorrect behavior by an employee of the Meurice.

"May we talk to her—Gabrielle?"

"It's her day off."

"That's right, I forgot. If you will just show us how to reach the *sortie de service*, we won't trouble you any more."

An elevator, spotless but plain, took them down to a dark corridor. From it they climbed narrow stairs to a doorway on the rue Mont Thabor. The guardian in his glass cage bowed to the assistant manager but looked at the intruders with irritation. More detectives! Across from the glass cage, only six feet away, were the time cards of the employees.

"Do you remember seeing Gabrielle leave last night?" Gordon asked.

"Gabrielle?"

"Gabrielle Soubiran," the assistant manager said.

"I must have seen her. I see everybody."

"What is she like?" It was only the second time his companion Perdoux had spoken. "Someone likely to break rules?"

The guardian shrugged.

"She is like the rest. Younger, of course. As for the rules, that's not my affair, except for the sortie and the time cards. I have repeated it several times today. No one left by this door. None but those who are authorized."

So now for the Sex Shop. His gaunt companion should at least know where the isolated Sex Shops were to be found. He could not imagine Randall patronizing those on the crowded rue St. Denis.

They found the right place on the second try, a cobblestoned street not far from the Gare St. Lazare. Not a sinister place now, in the sunny afternoon, with a boulangerie/patisserie on one side of the shop, a small bar on the other. Red and yellow lights framed the door, which was covered by a thick curtain. The window promised *Cuir Gadgets Video Rencontres* and prohibited the entry of those under eighteen. Inside, hundreds of cassettes covered the walls, classified as homosexual, lesbian, couples, bondage, sodomy. Large breasts, large behinds. Several tables were covered with colorful magazines.

Perdoux turned at once to the magazines. He picked up one called *Thai Lolitas*.

"The Swedish films are said to be the best. But for magazines, it is the Germans who excel."

"Keep looking at them," Gordon said quietly. "I'll try in back."

On a high platform near the front, from behind a glass

case containing many rubber instruments, the cashier watched them mournfully. A pock-marked Arab.

A dark door at the back of the shop led to the video cubicles: a sinister corridor. Near it, neatly ranged along the wall, was an inconspicuous but ample display of whips and chains. Seymour saw at once what he was looking for. The long metal bar with chains for wrists and ankles and the studded leather neck piece, spread out as for a crucifixion. Beside it was the torture instrument that also appeared in the FAX photograph: the set of rings for the penis, the circular metal weight as for an old-fashioned pharmacist's scale.

The cultural attaché tried to lift one of the wrist chains from its wall hook. The Arab approached.

"Permit me," he said. With a deft motion he freed the chain and put it in Seymour's hand. "The highest quality."

They were joined by Perdoux, who also felt the chain. He tried it on one of his bony wrists.

"It can be adjusted," the Arab said. "It is for you, the chain? You are the passive one?"

"I'm just looking." But Seymour said this in a way that suggested a serious customer, a student of refined pleasures. "How much is it?"

He silently translated the sum into dollars. Over a hundred and fifty.

"That's a lot!"

"For a new customer I can always make a price. For good will. You are American, no?"

"He's my friend," Perdoux said, smiling broadly. "A resident of Paris. He'll be back."

Seymour turned to the companion piece, with its apertures for both penis and testicles.

"And this one?"

"Very complicated. Nevertheless, you can have it for the same price."

"Do you rent?"

Something in Seymour's tone of voice awoke the Arab's wariness.

"That depends. There would have to be a good deposit."

"But you would rent to someone you knew well?"

The Arab frowned. Above him the skeletal Perdoux towered, no longer smiling.

"Why do you ask?"

"Did you rent these two machines to a friend recently?"

"You are wasting my time."

The Arab turned away, but Perdoux stopped him. Long bony fingers seized an elbow.

"Answer!" he shouted. The command *Réponds!* reverberated along the bright walls devoted to sensual pleasure.

"Let me alone! I'll call the police."

"We are the police," Perdoux said. He showed his card. "A little cooperation, please."

"I didn't rent them to anybody. I never rent. Ask any of my clients."

Perdoux, smiling again, slapped the Arab hard. The slap took Gordon back to a police interrogation of collaborators immediately after the liberation.

"Who was it?"

MINUTES LATER THEY WERE OUTSIDE the door of Luc's room. To their surprise it was unlocked. Even the Arab was surprised. Papers were scattered on the floor. Bondage magazines, comic books, clippings, snapshots, cassettes. A framed photograph, the glass cracked. A straight chair with one leg broken, as though smashed against a wall. The bed on which Randall had reclined in apparently blissful unconcern was still unmade. The television set had been overturned as by a thief enraged to find so little. The old television was not worth stealing.

They picked through the wreckage. An address book had been ripped in two but was perfectly legible. On one page there were only half a dozen names, spelled out in crude capital letters. Two caught Gordon's eye: GABRIELLE SOU-BIRAN, 6 septembre, probably a birthday reminder. The femme de chambre! The other, FRANÇOIS BOUQUILLON, *France-Soir*, 3500 francs. An address on the rue de Seine, not too far from his own apartment. He noticed the name because of a childhood memory of a French heavyweight champion, Moise Bouquillon. Not a very common name. His awakened instincts of the OSS days told him to trust such accidents.

And he knew even before looking whose face was on the framed photograph, staring playfully through the broken glass. It was an attractive face, youthful yet cunning. The young woman had stuck out her tongue in a child's gesture of saucy greeting. *Meilleurs souvenirs mon copain Luc,* and a scrawled *Gabrielle.*

"Can you get access to the Renseignements Generaux file right away?" Gordon asked.

"Of course."

"Let's see what you have on these two. Gabrielle Soubiran, François Bouquillon. Can you bring it to the Lutétia at seven?"

"Of course."

It was only ten minutes to six. They had been at work a little over an hour.

The Reception

The first meeting of the conference was further postponed, in deference to Randall's indisposition, but the reception went on as scheduled.

"We'll carry on as though nothing has happened," the chief security officer Chalmers said. "The Ambassador himself will drop in for a few minutes to greet the delegates."

To Gordon, the Lutétia looked like a military headquarters in a besieged city. The Boulevard Raspail entrance to the reception rooms was floodlit and ringed by police cars. Even the Central American ambassadors and honorary consuls and veterans of the diplomatic corps had to prove their identities and hold their hands above their heads while frisked. The official delegates had badges with miniature maps of the region overlaid by clasped hands. Some wore guayaberas, some linen suits and flowing ties. A few others were admitted to the crystal elegance of the Salle Babylone: the distinguished writers and painters in exile, and the politicians and aristocrats who were in peaceful opposition to their home regimes. One of these was the Cuban dentist Carlos Monzon.

In the lobby and the gilt corridor of perfume and jewelry showcases, held back by the French police but provided with a bar, were the run of the mill journalists and the photographers. All the rest, and the action committees in exile, were kept out on the sidewalk. The liberation fronts and brigades for national purification shouted slogans at the guests.

The Ambassador arrived in the company of his security officer and the CIA station chief Trent. His wife was suffering from a toothache and did not come.

"Who are all these people?" the Ambassador asked at the door to the main reception room. He observed with distaste four aged mariachis lounging near the bar, and the many guests with no ties and embroidered shirts that hung over their belts. "They look like ruffians."

The Ambassador took his place in a receiving line with the Costa Rican vice-chairman and the principal delegates. At his elbow was his security chief Chalmers, with his cultural attaché Gordon Seymour nearby to identify the exiled writers and painters and the few journalists admitted. But not many guests went through the line to hear the Ambassador's murmured greeting and meet his blue uncomprehending gaze. It was politically expedient, in times of ambiguity, to keep one's distance from the colossus of the north. Had there or had there not been a kidnapping? The press attaché Winton Miles, who hoped to placate those in the corridor, had moved from flat denial to a jocular "no comment." The story did not even merit a denial.

One of those who shook the Ambassador's hand was the dentist Dr. Monzon. He expressed a sympathetic interest in the ailing teeth of the Ambassador's wife.

"I treat many of your compatriots, your excellency. They are referred to me by the American hospital in Neuilly."

"Do you have a hygienist?"

"Of course."

"Many French dentists don't."

"I am not a French dentist, sir. I am a Cuban dentist."

"Oh."

At the conclusion of this conversation Dr. Monzon moved on to Gordon.

"Haven't I seen you in my office? You are the cultural attaché, no?"

"A root canal last year, very nicely done."

"And your Assistant Secretary who is indisposed, I hope he will be all right tomorrow. Sometimes this turmoil of the interior is nothing. Our Paris water is slightly laxative. But one must continue to drink water, preferably Perrier or Vitteloise. Fluid lost must be restored."

Gordon thought the dentist's expression peculiar, even mischievous, as though he were about to tell an off-color story.

"I'll try to remember your advice."

The Ambassador had made his courageous *acte de présence*. After ten minutes he left. Some bowed, some looked away. But once he was gone noisy conversations began. The Cuban ambassador embraced the greatest of the exile writers, as though to put art above politics, then castigated him loudly for his misstatements on prison conditions on the Isle of Pines. He had put too much faith in a deranged prisoner's recollections. A crippled veteran of the Farabundo Martí went after the Salvadoran consul general. When had the corrupt army chiefs ever kept their word? A veteran Sandinista poet accused the Honduran delegate of defending drug dealers. Presently everyone was speculating on the Assistant Secretary's absence and the rumor reported in *France-Soir*. Who would have kidnapped him, if that was what happened? There was much laughter. Even those most committed to Washington smiled. For decades they had suffered in silence the high moral rectitude of a succession of Assistant Secretaries and their chatter about free elections. It would not be entirely amiss for an Assistant Secretary to experience a little embarrassment. Could one believe the rumor of a chained man *in flagrante delicto*?

At the height of these discussions the old mariachis began to play. The brassy trumpet was punctuated by gasps.

To Gordon the strident voices and the mariachis brought back his two visits to Central America eight and ten years before. The room was filling with the smoke of the politicians' cigars and the pungent cigarettes of the writers and painters. In this haze he experienced a Proustian recall of not one but many odors. The smoking policemen and terror in blazing sunlight, the crouched Indians with their pitiful wares of chiclets and herbs, crawling cripples at the foot of the cathedral steps and the widows in black climbing them on their knees. The streets emptying at dusk, the loudspeakers and the sirens. And all the disappeared ones, the rector or senator or labor organizer who at this very moment might be hanging by his knees from the parrot's perch to await electric shocks or the metal grill of the *parilla* on sensitive parts. The Salvadoran Orden and D'Aubuisson's Arena, the Honduran COHEP and Guatemalan Mano vigilantes, the Medranos and Aranas and Paz Garcias, the *traficantes* and their private armies. They were all there, ghostly presences in the bright salon.

The cultural attaché felt a sharp twinge of guilt. Should he not have devoted himself all these years to the wretched down there, the abyss, rather than to the history and politics of France? He was one of the fortunate, exempted from horror. So too, standing a few feet away, were his three colleagues Chalmers, Trent the CIA station chief, Winton Miles the press attaché.

Gordon joined them.

The mariachis had begun to circle the room. The old trumpeter's cheeks bulged, his forehead was furrowed, he seemed ready to blow his last. No one was listening.

The CIA station chief put a friendly arm around Gordon's shoulder.

"So you haven't solved the mystery yet? Where is your Frenchman?"

"Perdoux? He's checking the files on the Meurice femme de chambre. He was supposed to be here at seven."

"Seems like a waste of time. What would a femme de chambre know?"

The dentist Dr. Monzon had just returned with a replenished glass. He was with Georges Langlade, a journalist well known to the American community. The journalist turned to the dentist with open mouth, as though expecting ministrations then and there. The dentist ignored him.

Monzon brought up again the problem of the Assistant Secretary's diarrhea.

"I said it was important to replenish the body's fluids. My friend Langlade reminds me that nothing is better for these horrors than a tisane. Or good old chicken soup. Do you expect Mr. Randall to be at the conference tomorrow?"

"I am confident he will be there," the security chief said.

Langlade, smiling, persisted.

"People are upset, of course, by the *France-Soir* story. Wouldn't it be better to acknowledge that some eccentric sent you a slice of erotica? You can say the face was indistinguishable. Pictures on a FAX are often blurred."

"There was no picture," Chalmers said. "A canard invented by *France-Soir*. Anything for a headline."

Langlade and Monzon moved a few feet away to join an old man with a stringy and soiled beard, once a luminary in the last cabinet of Batista and in exile since '59. Many years before Washington had given up its plan to install him as provisional president in a newly democratic Cuba. But he was still invited to the receptions.

Across the room the French agent Pierre Perdoux was approaching. He was a half hour late, but had paused long enough to get a glass of champagne at the bar. He held it awkwardly in his left hand while shaking hands with the three Americans.

"I excuse myself for being late. My search succeeded.

The Meurice femme de chambre Gabrielle Soubiran has an interesting history. She does not live at her address, no. Worse than that: she used to take vacations in disquieting places." He took no notice as Chalmers raised his right hand discreetly and put a finger to his lips. "Rumania, Bulgaria, even Sochi. She has had boyfriends of a doubtful ambiance. Several. I ask myself: Why does a femme de chambre vacation in Rumania? If tomorrow she doesn't come to work at the hotel..."

"Later," Chalmers whispered. "Tell us later."

But Langlade and Dr. Monzon had overheard. The journalist was drawn reluctantly back to the group, tugged firmly as by an invisible cord. The dentist had not moved. The bearded Batista veteran was relighting the stub of a cigar.

"What did you say about a femme de chambre?" Langlade asked.

"It's nothing. Naturally we do a security check on the employees of the hotel where Randall was staying. The Meurice. I was commenting on the femme de chambre for Mr. Randall's room. Just the usual waste motions."

"Waste motions?" Langlade said hoarsely. "What waste motions?"

At this point it occurred to Gordon to avail himself of Langlade's extraordinarily wide acquaintance among French journalists. He might know more than any computer.

"When I was a child I followed boxing very closely. I remember a French boxer with a strange name: Moise Bouquillon."

Langlade stared.

"A boxer? What's this about a boxer?"

"Just the name caught my eye. I wonder if you can tell me anything about a small-time newspaper man named François Bouquillon?"

Langlade dropped his glass. It did not break. Instead it rolled in the direction of Dr. Monzon and the old bearded exile. The glass came to a stop at the dentist's feet.

Langlade still did not move. He made no effort to retrieve his glass. The dentist also did not move.

"Are you all right?" Chalmers asked. "You don't look well at all."

"It is nothing," Langlade said weakly. "I also am nothing. I am an observer, only an observer."

Minutes later Langlade and Monzon left the room.

"What on earth was wrong with him?" Chalmers said. "*I also am nothing.* What a weird thing to say!"

An hour later Gordon and Perdoux, accompanied by the skeptical CIA station chief Trent, were in François Bouquillon's sixth floor miserable *chambre de bonne*. An unmade single bed, a bedside table covered with cigarette burns, a window near the sloping ceiling. No need to force the door or open it with plastic. Someone had already broken in. In place of family pictures or cheap Utrillo prints the walls were lined with photographs cut from sporting magazines and newspapers. A few were framed, most were tacked to the wall. Boxers at the end of a bout, with an eye closed or cheek bandaged, cyclists bent over like gnomes. Wrestlers in mid-air, leaping onto prone opponents. A goal-guard caught in the act of stopping the ball.

Gordon felt the same hand had been at work as in Luc's room above the Sex Shop: an overturned chair, a drawer and its soiled clothes on the floor, an empty bottle of Pernod on the bed, finished off by the intruder. Hundreds of racing programs and used parimutuel tickets tied in stacks by rubber bands, as though the expert on horse races and prizefights could not acknowledge having lost his bets. Letters of many years past pleaded for attention or offered advice, postcards showed soldiers and young women in innocent embrace, even a blue *poilu* from the first war with his arm around a boy of eleven or twelve, peaked face and foolish grin. The absent journalist and his soldier father? Shredded pages of computations all but covered the floor. *Turbigo, 6ème Chantilly, 2000 m., Robert 20,000 francs, Delille 15,000.* Were Robert and Delille the jockey and accomplice trainer of the horse *Turbigo*, promising a favorite would fail to rally in the stretch? Or jockeys of the two favorites, agreeing both should lose. Long lists of names were followed by numbers. These, Gordon surmised, were the recorded debts of years, collected by an obscure journalist with friends in all the *quartiers louches*. Payoffs accepted? assignations arranged? cocaine purchased, with initials only for the names? laundered money?

Somewhere in all the detritus there might be a document, a promissory note perhaps, linking François to Georges Langlade. Gordon felt this very strongly.

"There's nothing here," the CIA station chief Trent said. "Just a petty gambler and a cheap break-in."

Gordon did not agree. Long ago, 1944 in fact, in the just liberated city of Laval, he had been assigned the room vacated hours before by a German propaganda officer. There too the bed was unmade and a sickening perfume hung above it. On the desk were two books the officer had left behind in his hurried departure. One was a small volume of the poems of Heine, the other an album of photographs. Even before opening the album, which contained many pictures of dead French resistance fighters and of deportees getting onto trains, Gordon felt the presence of an almost palpable evil. He experienced the same nausea now, the

menace too, in the room of the journalist François Bouquillon. He would not have been surprised to find, with his
head in the toilet bowl, the drowned body of the taxi driver
Luc, in whose room the Assistant Secretary had been
chained. However, there was no toilet here, only a basin
with a single spigot. Under the bed, in fact, was a large white
chamber pot. In a building as old as this one there would
probably be small sit-down cubicles off the staircase, one for
each two floors.

"Petty and cheap, all right. But where is he? Looks to me
like whoever messed up the taxi driver's room has been here
too."

They went down the circling dark stairs, illuminated at
each floor by a small naked bulb of very few watts. Between
floors, and exhaling a subtle blend of turnip and licorice,
were the cubicles he had expected. But they were unoccu-
pied.

On the street floor, however, at the end of a corridor was
another toilet. It was a "Turkish" toilet, in a small dark
courtyard that also contained the bulging metal *poubelle* for
the building's garbage. A black hole in the stone floor, with
two raised slabs for the feet of the crouching person. The
courtyard was lit by a feeble bulb at the end of a string that
hung from a second-story window.

Behind the *poubelle* was a shed whose door was ajar. Inside
the shed was a body, not the body of the taxi driver Luc but,
it was fairly safe to assume, that of the late journalist François
Bouquillon.

The CIA station chief looked at Gordon admiringly. A
grudging admiration. But admiration nevertheless.

"You're in the wrong business," he said. "You ought to
be working for us."

* * *

TWO HOURS LATER, AND ALONE, Gordon was tired yet restless at the end of his long and altogether surprising day. He decided, before returning to his gloomy apartment on the rue Jacob, to walk along the Left Bank quays in the warm and pleasant summer night. Another time he would have relished sitting at one of the crowded cafés on the Place St. Michel, watching the intent tourists and the police working the suspect crowd of adolescents beside the fountain. But there had been enough excitement for one day, and he chose instead to descend to the cobblestone quays and follow them under the bridges and past Notre Dame in its pale white luminescence periodically flooded by the searchlights of the bateaux-mouches gliding out of the darkness beyond the Île de la Cité. The tourist boats followed each other like angry swans, the announcers flinging their commentaries against the brassy canned music of competitors. In one of the largest boats elegant diners slid by as on a moving stage, frozen in glittering silks. On shore, under the bridges, a few clochards huddled with their last bottle of the day. Near them lovers sat on the embankment, their legs over the side, staring up at the floodlit saints and gargoyles.

He walked on past the Pont de Sully, into the darkness where the first barges were tethered. The noise of the city was gone. Gone too the tedious bureaucratic questions, and the white and oddly scarred naked body of the journalist François Bouquillon that in a forensic examination revealed no wounds: only, as he had surmised, a death by drowning in human waste. Then an hour at the Embassy with Winton Miles, as the first crazy claims of responsibility reached the newspapers and television and the Embassy itself. An Italian red brigade once notorious for its kidnappings, Walloon activists who wanted only publicity, Basque separatists still dreaming of freedom from Spain. There would be several more absurd claims before the first serious demands came, from some French representative of a Colombian drug lord it might be, or even from Medellín itself. Or, looking eastward, from Teheran, Damascus or Beirut.

In the old days there were hundreds of barges, now only a few. Against the quay was a splendid well-lit barge, the *Zuider Zee* of Amsterdam, its brass rails polished, with flowers in the deckhouse windows. A table and chairs were set near the stern. On a reclining chair a burgher smoked his pipe at ease, fat legs outstretched. A dog slept at his feet. Beyond the *Zuider Zee* the barges were dark, with feeble riding lights and even the deckhouses dimly lit or with no light at all. Long ago, at a time of overwork, Gordon had daydreamed of a peaceful life on a French barge on the Canal du Midi, among the vineyards and the plane trees. Even to travel once in his life on one of the low-slung seagoing barges that hugged the coast, weathering the wild Bay of Biscay from San Sebastian and the Basque ports, their tanks filled with cheap brandy and cider from the apple orchards of northern Spain.

And here were two weather-beaten, rusted barges from the Basque country: the *Princessa* of Bilbao, the *Viscaya* of San Sebastian. Beyond them a larger barge floated a few feet offshore, though still moored to the quay: the *Don Carlos* of Santander. An odor of sardine and engine oil emanated from the *Princessa*, apparently from an open hatch, as though an enormous sick animal had breathed. Only a blue light in the deckhouse and the scratching of a poorly tuned radio. In the *Viscaya* a man with a beret was smoking in the dark while someone nearby snored. There were lights at two portholes just above the water line. But the glass was so filthy that nothing in the cabins could be seen.

The names *Don Carlos* and *Santander* teased and spun at the edges of his mind. Was the barge named for the old Don Carlos, the incorrigible Pretender of Joseph Conrad's romantic youth? And Santander? A city and port of northern Spain but also the name of a Cuban terrorist who was said to have died in Miami. Here too there were opaque lights at several portholes, but the deckhouse was dark.

He returned to the *Viscaya*. Would not an old barge on the Seine, moored to a quay traversed every day by hundreds of strollers, be the very last place a kidnapped dignitary would be hidden? And therefore, by extension, an excellent place to hide him?

Amused by this fancy, he thought to strike up a conversation with the smoking man in the deckhouse. He would begin by asking him if he had the correct time.

"Bonsoir, monsieur. Je regrette de vous déranger. Est-ce que vous avez l'heure?"

There was no answer.

Gordon persisted, speaking in a louder voice. Perhaps the silent smoker would enjoy talking about his home town. Or maybe it was only the home port of his old barge.

"Vous êtes de San Sebastian vous-même?"

This time there was a reply. It came in the sharp sound of a gun being readied. An old gun, Gordon suspected, even an old surplus piece from his own war or the Spanish civil war years before that.

He did not stop to ask.

AND IN THE LUXURIOUS OFFICE of Dr. Carlos Monzon, the dentist and the journalist Georges Langlade studied the illuminated map of Paris.

"What on earth has got into this old professor?" Monzon

said. "How could he possibly have known anything? Why doesn't he stick to cultural affairs?"

"I have nothing to do with it," Langlade said. "I'm getting out. Let somebody else get the great scoop."

"That would be out of the question, my friend. Once in, nobody gets out. Not even I, who wanted only to make the best possible arrangement for everyone concerned. Even for the misguided Assistant Secretary." The dentist stood up and pointed a long delicate finger at a spot far out in the wasteland of the thirteenth arrondissement. "For the moment it is obvious our wandering statesman must be moved again."

monday to friday

The Barge

THE ASSISTANT SECRETARY AWOKE, HIS head throbbing, to the peculiar sensation, not entirely unpleasant, of a cool wet cloth applied to long burns on his back. He was lying on his side on a coarse lumpy mattress and the wet cloth was being applied by a woman who whispered *doucement, doucement* as she followed the stripes of burn that crossed his back, first with the damp cloth, then with the soft tip of a finger. The Assistant Secretary thought he knew that voice. It was the femme de chambre Gabrielle and she was ministering to the red welts left by ten lashes of a horsewhip. They were on board the barge *Viscaya*, the very barge that would, a few hours later, attract the attention of Gordon Seymour.

Now fully awake, Randall turned to examine his surroundings. The mattress was only inches above the floor of a small, low-ceilinged cabin that smelled of burned oil and of something pungent and medicinal, a sweet yet sickening odor as of crushed or rotting apples. The room swayed gently as he surveyed it. Or was the swaying inside him? No table, one straight chair, a wall that curved inward oddly, with an opaque porthole near the ceiling. A sound of sloshing water.

The Assistant Secretary concluded that he was on some kind of boat. With another painful twist he looked up at the amused yet friendly face of Gabrielle.

"Be calm," she said, again using the familiar mode: *Restes tranquille*. "I will explain everything. We are prisoners on a barge attached to the quai next the Pont de Sully. During the day you were transported here in a box marked as perishable. All day you slept." She looked away from him with a thoughtful expression. "It is true, monsieur. All of us are perishable."

Was she making fun of him? Anger surged, then oddly faded, as though the hours of sedation had left him powerless.

"Who is on the barge?"

"Spanish types, but not the same Spanish types. The brute who whipped you is not on the barge. Not for the moment, anyway."

"The old bastard will rot in prison. For ten years, at least." He tried to sit up, and felt a sharp pain in his left ankle. The ankle was tied by thick cord to a rusted pipe that disappeared into the ceiling. "You, too, mademoiselle."

"Why didn't you tell him what he wanted?"

"He didn't ask anything. Just whipped."

"Lie down again," she said. "On the stomach this time, if possible. I will take care of you."

She dipped the cloth, a very dirty cloth, into a tin can, squeezed out some of the pungent liquid.

"What's that?"

"It is Calvados, but not French Calvados. The brandy of apples. This barge takes Spanish brandy to Chalons. It returns with wine, *Bourgogne supérieur* no doubt."

"You're rubbing me with brandy?"

"Why not? The alcohol stings. But also it disinfects. This barge is full of brandy. Do you like the brandy of apples? I think they will give us brandy to drink. All we want."

"How about untying my foot? That might take a year off your stay in prison."

"I will ask the men but not until I have established a rapport. For the moment I have no rapport with these Spaniards."

"In English we call that the shit of bulls."

"You still think I am not a victim?"

"Correct. I don't think you are a victim. Why aren't you tied up?"

She turned up the palms of her hands, hunching her shoulders in acknowledgment of the centuries of feminine privilege. This accentuated her breasts which, he surmised, would be soft and cool under the unspoiled summer blouse. For a moment he might have been back in his suite in the Meurice, appraising an attractive and possibly available femme de chambre.

"I am a woman."

"All right. So maybe you can get them to untie me. I will repeat my offer. Cooperate and you will be rewarded. My wife will pay you even if the Embassy won't."

The hand that had stroked his back impulsively touched his cheek. Almost a motherly gesture. He realized that he needed a shave.

"I will do what I can. I promise it. Soon you will understand that I am your friend."

"Not exactly," he said.

A bright yet streaked light appeared at the filthy porthole, moved across it, followed by another light. Simultaneously there was the sound of dance music, dance music of an earlier era, yet as loud as the music of today. The music drifted away, the darkness returned.

She went to the porthole.

"That was one of the bateaux mouches. However, it is impossible to see through this dirty window. Do you know about the bateaux mouches?"

He did not think this question worth an answer. He leaned forward to examine the rope around his ankle.

"The bateaux mouches take the tourists for promenades on the Seine. The best bateaux mouches begin at the Pont de l'Alma. From the boat you see Paris illuminated. The Place de la Concorde and the Chamber of Deputies, the Louvre, Notre Dame. On the return you see them in a different order: first Notre Dame, then the Louvre, then the Place de la Concorde. The boats that start from the Pont-Neuf are called Bateaux Vedettes. The new bridge *Pont-Neuf* is in fact very old."

"No kidding."

"If this window were clean I think you could see the back side of the Gothic cathedral Notre Dame. Illuminated. Notre Dame is like a ship riding on the river Seine."

"Where did you read that?"

"Be nice, monsieur. I am not like you a famous rich man with an education. You make fun of me? It is easy to make fun of a femme de chambre without parents."

She looked at him with her soulful brown eyes full of accusation. His scorn dissolved, if not his anger.

"All right, I'm sorry."

"You are sincere, monsieur? I hope so. You see, we have

to live together, here in this dirty cabin. It is better to be friends now, even if later you want to see me in prison."

The floodlight of another bateau mouche filled the porthole. A voice in German was explaining something on a loudspeaker that resonated badly.

"He is speaking in German," Gabrielle said, "For German tourists. The American tourists are more *sympathique.*"

Their conversation was interrupted by the sound of the door being unlocked. A burly man entered the room. He was wearing a black hood with holes cut for the mouth and eyes. He had half a baguette of bread and a milk bottle with water. He put the bottle and bread on the floor. With a sweeping gesture he commanded Gabrielle to follow him.

"Hop-la," he said. "The bitch comes with me."

"Please untie my friend," she said. "He won't run away."

"Shut your throat!"

He gave Randall's shackled foot a kick.

"Doesn't look like we'll be living together," Randall said.

"I will do what I can," Gabrielle said.

The hooded man kicked Randall again.

HE SLEPT. WHEN HE AWOKE the barge was underway and a milky daylight filled the porthole crusted with grime. He surmised he was near the stern, separated from the laboring engine by no more than a wall, since the cabin shook with its loud and pulsing vibrations. Even the steel pole to which his left ankle was attached vibrated. The regular grind and thrust of the engine was interrupted from time to time by a dull snapping, as of a connecting rod near the end of its days.

There was water on the floor. And the water of the Seine, he trusted it was still the Seine, sloshed by just beneath the filthy porthole. His mattress, he surmised, must be a foot or two below water level, the porthole a few feet above it.

His musings were interrupted by Gabrielle, brisk and smiling, with a tin cup of coffee and a small piece of bread, also a chamber pot. She put the chamber pot near the head of his mattress as nonchalantly as a Meurice femme de chambre replacing a porcelain ashtray.

"You are famous, monsieur. There is talk of you all morning on the radio. I think your picture will be on the cover of the illustrated weekly magazines."

He took a sip of the coffee, which was sickly sweet. He spat it out. The coffee soaked his workman's blouse.

"What's in this?"

"The apple brandy. Without it the coffee is undrinkable."

She sat down at the foot of the bed and examined the bound ankle. She rubbed it gently.

"Your poor ankle," she said. "I will insist they take the rope off. It is enough to lock you in."

He made himself drink a little of the coffee. Was he being drugged again? It probably didn't matter so long as there were no more whips.

"What are they saying?"

"Your President is outraged. Otherwise he has no commentary."

"What else?"

"There are absurdities. People say they have you—terrorists, several terrorist groups in fact. Some crazy people from Belgium claim they have you, they ask for money. But we know you are here on a barge with three Spanish. You know where we are on the Seine? We are going up the river, not down the river to Rouen and Le Havre."

"What else? Try to remember what they're saying."

"I will tell you. The French are looking for you everywhere. The trains, the airports, all the highways. The slums of the Arabs, the cafés of the gangsters. But not the boats on the Seine! Here we are only ten or twenty kilometers out of Paris, we move slow as a tortoise and they don't look in the boats." She reached for his tin cup, took a sip of the coffee, grimaced. "However, I think today they will find us. The police say they make progress. Perhaps today at last they will think to look at the boats."

"I doubt it. What else was there on the radio?"

"A big shot intellectual, I forget his name, he speculates. Who will want the American Assistant Secretary? Who will buy him? For one, Heptolla. Terrorists in Beirut."

"Hezbollah." Randall made the correction with distaste. Until now he had resisted seeing himself in an Iranian or Lebanese cell, or in any worse predicament than his present one. The rope attached to his ankle suddenly felt like a heavy chain. He could be tortured, there could be worse than whips. "What else?"

"Some South Americans. Columbia, the kings of the drug. Medalo, he says."

The aftertaste of the coffee became even more sickening.

"Medellín. Listen, Gabrielle, all that is impossible. This is a small affair, very small, nothing to do with the big terrorists. Just some amateurs with an old barge. So it was first you and the taxi driver and then somebody took over from you. Who did?"

"Believe me, monsieur. I know nothing. The participation of Luc and me, that was a mistake. I am in accord with you about that. The Spaniards they captured you, they captured me. What happened to Luc? Maybe they killed him. All I know is that it is Spaniards. The old man who whips you, he is a Spaniard. The three men on this boat, they are Spaniards. I do not think they are evil men, just brutes. They are not the criminals. They are paid by the criminals to keep us, that is all."

"There's something else you're not telling me."

Her eyes glazed with tears. He had the impression she could produce them at will.

"The radio says somebody killed a friend of Luc. François Bouquillon, a journalist. Luc went to him for information and now he is dead. I think Luc too is dead."

Randall found this new development very disturbing.

"Luc was trying to sell me to a journalist François, and this François wouldn't buy? So Luc killed him?"

"No, no, no! Luc wanted only information. He wanted to know who you were. He should have said, *'Gabrielle, we have made a big mistake. This is a political man, very important. We must take him back to the Hotel Meurice. Right away.'* Only he did not say that, Luc." She wept quietly. "Last year we went to the obstacle races at Auteuil with François. The big favorite I bet on fell at the last obstacle and the horse doctors they came and looked at my horse and they shot him. But I did not get my money back. If your horse is dead you should get your money back."

"Which one are you crying about? François or the horse?"

"For François. He was an ugly man but I believe his intentions were good." She dabbed at her eyes. "My intentions also were good, more or less. We just thought you were a rich industrial whose enterprise would not miss a little money. A few thousand francs."

The weeping resumed. He wanted, absurdly, to touch her wet cheek. To console her.

"All right, Gabrielle. I'll try to believe you are just a little fool who made a big mistake. So now I want you to listen carefully to everything the men say and everything you hear on the radio. We must get out of this together."

Her face brightened. She picked up his right hand and held it against her cheek. Gently but firmly she rolled his hand until it rested against her mouth. From what movie had she picked up that? His renewed anger vanished at the touch of her mouth.

"I knew you would understand! Today when we are rescued I hope you will explain that I too am a victim."

They were not rescued on that first day on the river, Tuesday, nor on the days that followed. The barge lumbered past Corbeil, Melun, and the forest of Fontainebleau, not far from the castle itself. Here, Gabrielle explained, were many souvenirs of the emperor Napoleon, also of the gracious and beautiful Marie Antoinette. She herself had stood there for many minutes, admiring the golden boudoir of Marie Antoinette, although the guide kept urging her to stay with the group. Even earlier than that, as a child in fact, she had played among the wild rocks in the forest of Fontainebleau.

"I cut my foot on a rock. Otherwise it is a day I will never forget."

On the evening of the second day the barge entered the narrow Canal de Loing, leaving the ruffled waters and traffic of the Seine. The Basques (that was what the Spaniards said they were) no longer let her listen to the radio. They would tell her what she needed to know, her questions made them nervous. On the other hand they had become more agreeable and invited her to have dinner with them, rough food but nourishing, a *blanquette de veau* cooked several days before, with potatoes that had acquired the consistency of soup. Randall could hear all four laughing as they ate. They had taken off their black hoods, except when they went to his cabin. Whenever the barge neared a lock, they put Gabrielle in with him.

She was allowed to take a portion of the veal stew to the Assistant Secretary, also a glass of red wine and a glass of brandy. Everyone drank a lot of the apple brandy, the men straight, hers mixed with water. There was a shortage of drinking water but no shortage of brandy. They knew how to tap the tanks.

"You seem to be pretty good friends with them," he complained.

"It is essential. One must do what one can to have the little comforts. They wanted to give you only bread, I got you the *blanquette de veau*."

On the third day she even won permission for him to spend several hours in a better cabin on the other side of the barge. Here she and two of the crew slept by turns. There was an armchair, and the worn sofa had soft cushions. Here too he was tied to a metal pole extending from floor to ceiling, but he could move about and even look out a clean porthole at the peaceful borders of the canal. The towpath was almost covered with grass and shaded by plane trees and poplars in neat rows. A fisherman slept beside his propped up pole. Another walked along the towpath, reading, followed by a small dog. Even the laboring engine seemed quieter here. Whenever they approached a lock they were returned to the first cabin. Then Gabrielle too was a prisoner. They sat side-by-side on the mattress, listening to the filling or emptying waters of the lock, as the barge slowly rose or fell.

"I would like to pass my old age as a lockkeeper on a canal," she said. "The wife of a lockkeeper, that is."

"You'd be bored to death."

"Not at all. I would read and listen to the radio and look at television. And dream. I would like to spend my old age dreaming. First the adventures, then the dreams."

After a long wait at a lock where the crew took on pro-visions, also two newspapers, Gabrielle came to him with questions. It appeared the men were puzzled by what they read. She believed they expected instructions and had re-ceived none.

"They say you detest the communists. Why is that? What did they ever do to you, the communists? I think there are very few of them left."

"They wanted to destroy us. Our markets, our bases. Our values."

"That is ridiculous, you have been misinformed." He laughed but she persisted. "I have been to the peaceful communist countries for vacations. Rumania, Bulgaria, Russia. However, they are no longer so peaceful. The hotels are not the Meurice but they are inexpensive. Big swim-ming pools. Also I had a communist lover, a student at the Sorbonne who gave speeches at the Palais de la Mu-tualité. He was very nice but he talked too much. Even in bed he talked."

"What did he talk about?"

"I have no idea, I was not listening. At last he finished his studies and went to Marseille. Often I regret our vacations together. Yugoslavia was the best. Dubrovnik, also Hvar." Her distant gaze focused on the lost student, then returned to himself. The brown eyes were friendly and speculative. "I would love to have a vacation with you, monsieur. I could learn so much. In turn I could teach you the history of France. Louis Quatorze, the two Napoléons, Charles de Gaulle."

"How about Mitterand?"

"He is less interesting."

* * *

LATE THAT AFTERNOON A LONG black Mercedes with opaque windows appeared on the towpath and followed the barge, flashing its lights. The barge drifted to a stop and a man and woman, both in white coats and wearing masks, came on board. Each was carrying a doctor's bag. They conferred briefly with a member of the crew, the man in the white coat speaking Spanish, then came to the cabin where the Assistant Secretary was reluctantly listening to Gabrielle's detailed account of a movie she had seen the week before.

The man was of medium height with dark hair and olive skin. The woman was stocky and blonde, with the broad shoulders and square jaw of a professional athlete, a wrestler perhaps. The man glanced at Gabrielle and asked her to fetch a basin of water. Clean water. It was a voice with a burr, not quite French, but not Marseillais either. While Gabrielle was gone the two visitors opened their bags. In one were bottles and vials, syringes, needles, scissors and knives. The man unfolded a clean white cloth and laid it on the mattress. The woman's bag also contained bottles and scissors, and what appeared to be a hair dryer.

"What's going on?" Randall said. "Please untie this rope—"

"That's unnecessary," the doctor said in English. "Just a few precautions."

"I will personally guarantee you fifty thousand dollars to get me out of here and to the United States Embassy in Paris. You can hold me in your car while a courier gets the money."

The doctor hardly appeared to be listening. He took a bottle and an exceptionally long and fat syringe from the bag, also what appeared to be a square pad of ink. Was he a veterinarian hired to do whatever he had to do? Not a real doctor?

"There will be no charge for this injection. Roll up your sleeve."

"I don't know what these people are paying you. I can guarantee you twice the amount. Help me and you won't go to prison."

The doctor said nothing. Gabrielle returned with the basin of water. He handed her a small pill bottle.

"Give him three a day with the meals. Not before them."

"I'm *not* having an injection," Randall said.

"Get one of the men," the doctor said to Gabrielle. "No, two of them." He slapped his hands, hard, to accentuate the command.

"He doesn't need that," Gabrielle said. "He will tell you what you want to know. He is a reasonable man who recognizes what is possible."

"Shut up and get the men."

They rolled up his left sleeve.

"First the thumb print. Please do not resist." With a quick motion he seized Randall's right hand, then the thumb, and placed it carefully on the ink pad, then cleaned the thumb with alcohol. Not only the tip of the thumb. Cleaned the whole thumb.

Two of the crew members appeared at the door, wearing their hoods. With a wave the doctor dismissed Gabrielle. They pushed her out and locked the door. The woman in the white coat did not watch. She was leaning over her open bag, deciding what to use.

"Now for the injection, Mr. Randall. Just a precaution. A little summer malaria. Against *paludisme*, uncomfortable but not always fatal."

"That's crazy, there's no malaria in France."

"Have you studied medicine?"

He rubbed the Assistant Secretary's arm with alcohol, just above the elbow."

"You'll get twenty years, you're making a terrible mistake."

The doctor laughed.

"It's you who made the mistake, Mr. Randall."

"Leave him alone!" Gabrielle screamed from behind the locked door.

THE ASSISTANT SECRETARY WOKE TO a dull throbbing pain in his left hand and a peculiar tickling of the scalp, as though ants had taken up residence there. But it was his right hand, the thumb to be exact, that was thickly bandaged from a stubby tip to its junction with the index finger. The pain shifted from the untouched left thumb to the bandaged one. The bandage, which did not look very professional, had a small red stain near the tip. A medicinal odor, an odor that was also a taste, seemed to rise from within him rather than from the outside. He wanted to vomit. He tried to suppress the image of a package opened to disclose an ear, then the far more disturbing image, memory rather, of mutilated corpses left to rot on the debris-strewn slopes of the volcano in Salvador. A perverse attraction for a certain class of tourists, a warning for native subversives. The special envoy, not yet an Assistant Secretary then, had expressed his distaste for these methods to the then Minister of Justice, a cultured but resigned man. But war was war. The Minister of Justice had shrugged his shoulders. Randall did not want to think of that now.

He looked at his thumb. Why wasn't the thumbprint enough? Enraged, he crawled to the end of his chain and pounded on the locked door. And shouted for help, in French, in English, in Spanish.

Minutes later one of the hooded men unlocked the door. Gabrielle was admitted. She was carrying a glass of dark liquid, presumably brandy. She inspected the bandage.

"Your poor finger!" she said. "And I thought it was the police saving us when I heard people come on board!"

"It's not a finger. It's my *thumb*, what's left of it."

"The horrible doctor assured me he took only a small slice. In time you will be back to normal. Almost, that is." She touched his cheek gently, then, as though reluctantly, looked higher. And began to laugh. "Oh my God! What in God's name have they done? All they said was a little haircut."

He started to feel his hair with the bandaged hand, then rubbed it with his left. Much of the hair was gone. But what was left was in small stiff yet oily ringlets. Hundreds of stiff curls.

"You poor little one. They have made you look like a girl! No! More like an old woman, one who is going bald. It is the color of old women who have dyed their hair too often."

"They dyed it?"

"Reddish brown." She felt the curls, rubbing them between thumb and index finger. "One will get used to it in time. When we are liberated you can return to your own color. Or perhaps you will choose something more becoming."

"Shit," he said. *Merde*.

She laughed.

"That is what in France we call the word of Cambronne. I think he was one of Napoléon's generals. When the general discovered that all was lost he was asked for his opinion and all he could think of was to say that."

"I'm not in the mood for historical anecdotes."

She laid her hand on his cheek. The hand was soft and cool.

"Please pardon me, I never think before I speak. I wanted only to take your mind off your troubles. Cambronne, that was long ago." She caressed his cheek, then ran her fingers lightly over his new curls. "It is not totally disagreeable, that it makes you look like a woman. Would you like me to come to you tonight? It is the least I can do. We will sleep here together, though the bed is very small."

The proposal seemed too ridiculous to answer. Would his kidnapper next propose that he get her a green card and an apartment on Capitol Hill for their trysts?

She did better. She had him moved to the other less suffocating cabin, with his ankle attached to the pole by a longer rope. The soft stir of the canal water was lulling. He fell asleep to the sound of radio music from the deckhouse, and the coarse voices of the sailors interrupted from time to time by Gabrielle's good-natured laughter.

THIS TIME HE WOKE TO the tingling and pleasant sensation of a damp cloth caressing his chest. He was all but naked, only his shorts and socks remained. It was morning. The porthole was open a few inches, and pale sunlight brushed the almond hair of Gabrielle leaning over him.

"What day is it?"

"Friday. Lie still and enjoy your bath," she said. "I have washed your clothes and hung them next to the engines. In a few hours they will be dry."

She was sitting at the edge of the bed. On the floor beside her was a pail, also a dark unlabeled bottle.

"More brandy?"

"First I wash with water, then the brandy to stimulate."

It seemed pointless to resist. And the water was deliciously cool. First the damp cloth, then her fingers soft as the touch of a spider or moth. She took the lobe of his right ear between her thumb and index finger, rubbing gently, then leaned forward as though to put it in her mouth.

"You permit? This is one of the six zones of pleasure. There is a channel of sensation from the ear to the penis. Suck the ear, the penis responds."

She licked the earlobe gently, then took it in her mouth and sucked. At once his bandaged thumb experienced a sharp pain, followed by a slow throbbing. The penis was unaffected.

"Did you like that?" She spilled a few drops of brandy, first on one nipple, then the other. "This also is a zone of pleasure. The channel passes through the appendix. Have you lost it, the appendix?"

Using both index fingers she circled the nipples, one finger going clockwise, the other in the opposite direction. This time there was a faint stirring somewhere in the area of the loins, but with the third circling of the nipples the bandaged thumb again began to hurt. Was it infected? At the thought his flicker of desire vanished.

"That hurts."

"Hurts? That is impossible! Let me try here."

She probed with an index finger near the appendix, as though searching for an operation scar, then pushed in, hard. This time it might have been a needle that probed, under the bandage.

"It's my thumb that hurts. Let's forget the other zones."

Using both hands she slipped off his shorts. She picked up his limp member in order to bathe it. Slowly it stiffened, but the pain in the thumb returned. By now, however, resistance seemed useless. Tomorrow he could belabor her with accusations. Today he was ready to accept small mercies.

"This is like fresh young asparagus," she said, fondling the awakened member. "Do you like asparagus? In France we have both the green and the white. At its best asparagus is firm and crisp, yet soft as silk after peeling of the outer skin." The pain in the bandaged thumb became worse. "Which do you prefer, monsieur? The green asparagus or the white?"

"You're crazy," he said. "You ought to be locked up, and not just for kidnapping people."

She laughed, brushed his forehead with a kiss. She began to remove her blouse.

"It is hot on this barge so I wear no brassiere. For lingerie and jewels the Galéries Lafayette is best. But for food I prefer the Bon Marché at Sèvres Babylone. Do you know the Bon Marché?"

Her breasts were larger than he expected. He was tempted to touch one.

"At the Bon Marché they do marvels with almond paste. They even make tennis balls out of almond paste." She picked up the member again. And squeezed. It was becoming firm at last. With the other hand she explored his balls. "These are like the best prunes, sometimes bursting with ripeness, at other times they are wrinkled and hard."

"My thumb hurts."

"Keep your mind on agreeable experiences. Have you had roast goose stuffed with prunes and foie gras? I can make it. First the prunes are soaked in hot water, then the pits are removed."

Her hand continued its activity. It appeared to be moving in time with her words, although her mind was clearly elsewhere. A squeeze, hesitation, another squeeze. He tried to sit up, but she pushed him down. She removed the rest of her clothing.

"The best bread in Paris is Polain," she said. "On the rue du Cherche Midi. The best ice cream in Paris is Bertillon. That you can have in all of the good cafés and restaurants."

Contemplatively, moving as slowly as a person stirring in sleep, she twisted until her left knee was against his hip and her right knee was in place on the other side.

"Is that quite comfortable?" she asked.

"You're still going to prison."

"I am sick of the *blanquette de veau*. I long for a good dinner. The day we are rescued we will have a great meal. We will begin with oysters, which are known to be aphrodisiacs. Then *ris de veau* or perhaps a nice lobster. Today I think we are rescued."

"You talk too damn much," he said.

She began to move above him, up and down, in a gentle and meditative manner.

"If we are not rescued we must rescue ourselves. I will arrange something."

Escape

She decided to get the crew drunk.

It was already dusk, with the *Viscaya* tied up for the night, when she left the Assistant Secretary's bed. The three Basques were playing cards in the deckhouse and drinking apple brandy. A wailing accordion reached them from the radio in the galley. One of the men was already half drunk and singing raucously. A greasy roast chicken lay in pieces as though torn apart by hand. Beside it was a cornucopia of cold *frites*. There was no sign of a knife.

Two rows of poplars followed the canal's gentle curve and disappeared into a blue evening mist. There were no lights anywhere, other than the riding lights of the barge and the feeble bulb by which they were playing cards. But soon there would be a full moon, in less than an hour perhaps.

"Where did you get the chicken?"

"At the last lock. Serve yourself, little one."

Sers toi, petite! The familiar form was affectionate, as though she were already one of them. She was not a real prisoner, only a poor femme de chambre who had stumbled into an affair involving the rich and the great ones. She was an innocent, really. Everyone makes mistakes.

"Isn't there any wine? With chicken there should be wine, preferably white."

"What's wrong with the brandy?"

She shrugged.

"The wineskin you showed me. Can one drink brandy from it?"

The three men looked at each other and laughed.

"Why not?"

One of the men left the table. He returned with the old wineskin filled with brandy. While he was gone she picked up the cards and showed them a trick. She undid the top button of her blouse and slipped a card under it, a king, then plucked the same card from behind the ear of the man named Esteban. Her fingers did a delicate erotic dance, just touching an ear lobe of each of the men in turn. The man named Pedro had an earring on his left ear. She pulled it.

The man with the wineskin handed it to her. He showed her how to hold it. She kept her tongue in place, allowing only a little of the brandy to trickle through.

"You're cheating," the man named Pedro said. "You're not drinking."

"I am a woman. It is the men who drink in an admirable fashion. I would like to see each of you drink from the wineskin in the manner of a man. A real man of the Basque country, keeping the tongue out of the way, the throat open. Which of you can drink the most?"

"We are brothers," Pedro replied. "We drink the same."

"Nevertheless it would be amusing to see which can drink the most tonight. Life is very boring on this barge. It is only a game, something to pass the time."

"And you, little one?"

"I will dance. Change the radio for better music. I will dance while you drink. I will take off the blouse when the first wineskin is finished, then the skirt when the second is finished. After that we will see."

An hour later she returned to Randall, buttoning the blouse, and untied the ankle attached to the pole. He could hear the drunken shouts of the men, but muffled, as though coming from under a blanket.

"I have locked the pigs up. They are in the kitchen, drunk as clochards. Soon they will fall asleep."

For the moment, however, they were shouting.

"We must get off the barge before anyone hears them. How is your thumb?"

"Infected, no doubt."

"Tonight when we find a comfortable hotel I will make you a new bandage. We will have a nice big bed with clean sheets and a hot bath and tomorrow you will telephone to your friends in Paris."

"Tonight. Not tomorrow."

"They will come to get you in an expensive car. Why not a Rolls? Tell them you want a Rolls. You will explain that I too am a victim. Also that you and I are now friends. You are in accord?"

"I'm not promising anything. First let's get to a telephone."

They jumped to the towpath, first Gabrielle, then the Assistant Secretary. There were no lights in any direction, only the lights of the barge, and the white full moon hovering above the thick woods beyond the poplars. An owl hooted. Far off a dog barked, twice.

"We must get away from the canal before the men break out."

"They won't break out," she said. "Soon they will be asleep."

They walked rapidly along the towpath, south. The last lock in the direction of Paris was far behind them, no point in going back. A signpost, slightly askew, pointed to a dirt road leading away from the canal and into the woods. He could just make out the words: AU MOULIN. Not the name of a village, but at least a mill meant human habitation, lights, possibly a telephone.

The road dwindled to grassy ruts, as though no car had traversed the wood for many months. A break in the woods, and they could see each other in the moonlight, then darkness. They held hands, feeling their way.

"Where is the damned mill?" Gabrielle said. "In school we read a book about a mill called *Lettres de Mon Moulin*. By Alphonse Daudet."

"How did you like it?" the Assistant Secretary asked absently. His mind was on other matters. In an hour he would be free. In fact he was already free. So the time had come to think carefully about explanations to be made, first to the Embassy and the department, then to the press. Eventually to his wife.

"Very boring."

They came into a moonlit clearing and saw the windmill,

one of its arms missing, and beyond it two dark stone houses very low to the ground.

"This mill is abandoned," Gabrielle said. "What is a mill doing here in the middle of a horrible forest?"

The door to the mill was open, appeared to be missing in fact. A thick guano paste shone on the floor illuminated by the brightening moon. There were rustlings in the darkness above. An owl hooted, followed by a wild fluttering. A bat rushed past them out the door, then several bats.

They returned to the towpath and continued south, following the curving canal. Presently they came to another sign, LA MORINIERE, pointing to a somewhat more promising dirt road. A second sign warned gypsies to stay away. STATIONNEMENT INTERDIT AUX NOMADES. Twenty minutes walking brought them to an asphalt road, and moments later to a cluster of stone houses and a few lights, even a two-story building announcing itself as CAFÉ TABAC. Just beyond the village, on a moonlit hilltop, was a small chateau or a rich man's summer residence. There, if not here in the CAFÉ TABAC, would be a telephone and creature comforts, even a sitdown toilet. But the chateau was dark. If there were lights in the chateau, they were on the other side.

The one small room of the café was filled with the raw smoke of cigarettes. There were three rough tables of oak. At one table were two tall black men oddly garbed in white robes, at a second three sturdy peasants with berets. Could they have fallen in with more Basques? No one spoke or even looked at them. Behind the bar with its zinc counter another peasant wearing a beret stared at them sullenly: the propietor no doubt, bartender and proprietor both. Above the bar were three framed pictures. Two of them were portraits of black men. To Randall the faces looked vaguely familiar.

They sat down at the third table. Gabrielle ordered a glass of white wine, the Assistant Secretary a beer.

"It's too late," the bartender said. "The café is closed."

"I want to use the telephone. I have to call Paris."

"What are you? You have a funny voice."

"American."

"Please serve us, monsieur. This American is a very important man. Give him his beer, me a glass of dry white wine, a Pouilly perhaps. Then he will go to the telephone."

The bartender scrutinized Randall's rumpled workman's clothes. Even Gabrielle was a bit disheveled.

"Show your money first."

"There's been an accident. We were kidnapped, to tell you everything."

The bartender laughed.

"So you don't have any money? Is that it?" He jerked a fat thumb in the direction of the door. "Don't come back."

"I want to telephone the American Embassy in Paris," Randall said. "Collect."

"Collect! You think they will listen to scum like you?"

Randall told himself it was important to keep his temper. Behind the bartender was a mirror and in it he saw the two blacks in their white robes, staring at him. What were they? He looked again at the two framed portraits above the mirror and recognized the two faces. Official portraits such as in the old days would be found in many stores and houses in Port-au-Prince. Benevolent faces.

François Duvalier, Papa Doc. His son and heir Jean-Claude Duvalier, Baby Doc. He had met both, the father for ten minutes at a reception in the white palace in Port-au-Prince, the son years later. At the latter meeting he was among those persuading the fat young dictator to go into exile. He could live in luxury abroad, he and his beautiful Michèle, though not in the United States. He would have to spend his millions in France.

He turned to look at the two tall blacks in the white robes. It was now obvious they too were Haitians, responsible no doubt for the presence of the pictures.

"Why are the Duvaliers here?" Randall asked them. "What are they doing in this café?"

"How do you know who they are?" The voice was languorous yet threatening. First one, then the other black man stood up. They were very tall. Both faces had several scars, one of the men had lost an eye. "What does shit like you know about the Duvaliers?"

It seemed time to show his cards.

"I am the Assistant Secretary of State Thomas Randall."

Everyone in the room laughed, everyone but Gabrielle.

The proprietor came out from behind his counter, still laughing.

"Take your madman away," he said, giving Gabrielle a fatherly pat. "Take him back to his hospital."

"It's true what he's saying, monsieur. Just let him use the telephone, then you will see. You will regret your bad manners."

"First show me your money."

"We were robbed."

One of the black men dismissed the bartender with a rough wave. The French peasants at their table did not move.

"An instant, please." He addressed Randall more politely. "What do you know about the Duvaliers?"

"What do you want to know? Both proclaimed themselves Presidents-for-Life. The father François, who was once a doctor, is dead, the son Jean-Claude is now living with his wife Michèle in Vallauris near Cannes. I've met them both."

"Where did you stay in Port-au-Prince?"

"The first time in a villa in Pétionville, the second time at the Habitation Leclerc."

The interrogator turned to the proprietor.

"Let him telephone Paris. This man is no clochard."

The telephone was behind the counter. Everybody listened. After a quarter hour's confusion Randall reached the Embassy night operator, identified himself as the kidnapped Assistant Secretary, and asked to speak to the security officer on duty.

The operator laughed, said he was not authorized to accept collect calls and hung up. A second effort produced the same result.

"That's enough," the proprietor said. "Get the impostor out of here before I call the police."

"Please do call the police," Randall said. "Right away."

"There are no police here." He was losing patience. He began to push Randall toward the door. "Enough of this foolishness. Get him out of here. Out!"

One of the tall Haitians gave the propietor a push in turn. He retreated behind his counter. The three peasants at the other table were keeping out of it.

"I think there is something here," the Haitian said. "Something a little disquieting. I think we will take him to the chateau for a few questions. The maître will know what to do with him."

THEY WERE TAKEN TO THE chateau in a stretch limousine. The two men in the front seat wore army fatigues. The one who was not driving had a submachine gun slung over his shoulder. At the gate to the castle and also at the front door were more tall blacks in army fatigues. They snapped to attention when the Haitians in white robes descended. Their revolvers and the beads of their cartridge belts glittered in the moon-light. Their eyeballs shone.

The large entrance hall was cold and damp and poorly lit by a chandelier with bulbs missing or dark. At the foot of the stone stairway a large white hound appeared to challenge them, staring, then turned and stalked off down a dark hall. There were chicken droppings at many places on the stone floor.

"You will meet the boss. His name is Hypollite Jasmin. You are to address him as 'Maître'. You can speak French. Speak to him in French." He turned to Gabrielle. "You will stay silent."

The name Hypollite Jasmin revolved unpleasantly in the Assistant Secretary's groping memory. A high officer of the dreaded Tonton-Macoutes? Chief of the military barracks adjoining the Presidential Palace in Port-au-Prince? An aide-de-camp of the President who tortured a deputy to death after one of the aborted coups? Obviously he was one of those who had gone into exile with Baby Doc.

They were escorted up the stone stairway, at the top of which another white hound awaited them. The dog sniffed, growled, and turned away in contempt. Then a brightly lit Louis XVI salon, fauteuils whose arms were worn to threads of silk, a Savonnerie carpet with chicken droppings. A large white chicken was roosting on the back of one of the fauteuils. The chicken appeared to be watching him.

"Remain standing until the master asks you to sit down."

"I do not like these Haitians," Gabrielle said as soon as they were alone. "I think they are terrorists."

"Don't worry. They're only underlings."

The Assistant Secretary was noted for the firmness of his attitude in dealing with terrorists, but for the moment he was almost sick with what he acknowledged was plain fear.

He sat down on one of the fauteuils. A silken armrest at once gave way. He tried to fit it back.

Twenty minutes later Hypollite Jasmin appeared, buttoning his trousers. The trousers were ordinary denim but his white coat was decorated with medals. It too he proceeded to button, using his left hand. The right hand was withered or perhaps disfigured by torture. The eyes were small and furtive, the hair cropped very short. Randall thought he knew that face, perhaps from a moment's meeting in Port-au-Prince, perhaps from photographs. The face was above all memorable by the many gold teeth, two of which protruded over the lower lip. It was the mouth of a patient who took pride in the quantity of gold.

The two men with white robes stood guard nearby. One had a large revolver.

"Call me maître," Hypollite Jasmin said. "What are you doing in La Morinière? The village is private property, you have no business here. What do you want?"

The Assistant Secretary explained the circumstances of his kidnapping, from his innocent desire to walk about Paris alone to their escape from the barge *Viscaya*. He omitted the details of the compromising photograph. The Haitian punctuated Randall's narrative with jerky nods and an occasional horrible smile.

"I don't believe any of this," he said. "Maybe you are a CIA interfering in my affairs? Is it perhaps that, the truth? No American diplomat would ever wear clothes like that. Not to mention the hair."

"They cut my hair. A woman cut the hair. A man cut my thumb. A Spaniard, I think. The men on the barge were Basques."

"Call me maître."

"I'm sorry, *maître*. I would like to phone the Embassy."

"You tried at the café. They would not accept your call. You are an impostor."

"He is telling you the truth, maître. I, Gabrielle Soubiran, am the innocent accomplice in an event I will regret for the rest of my life. I, like you, thought he was an ordinary man. But no. He is what he says he is."

"There is said to be a famous photograph of a poule sucking the penis of the Assistant Secretary of State. That is you, perhaps? Turn around and let me see your back side. Show me your carte d'identité."

"We have nothing, maître. No carte, no money, nothing. In Paris the Spaniards took everything. Telephone the Hotel Meurice. Ask them if there isn't a femme de chambre named Gabrielle Soubiran who didn't return to work. She's a victim herself, knows she made a mistake. As for the photograph, I was in no position to resist."

Hypollite Jasmin turned to Randall with renewed interest. He was beginning to believe.

"Let us for the moment accept your story. In time we can verify. If you are Thomas Randall why did you betray the President-for-life Jean-Claude Duvalier at the time of the exodus? He is a freedom fighter. All his benevolent life he has fought the communists. You too, if you are really Thomas Randall, you too fought the communists. The President is a man of good will who bows to necessities. All he asked was to keep a little of his money and to be allowed to live in a fine house in New York City among his friends. Instead you would not accept us. You condemn us to live among the stupid French. I, Hypollite Jasmin, I wanted only an apartment on the Park Avenue in New York. A modest apartment. Why did you exclude us?"

Gabrielle looked at Randall as though also to ask, *Why?*

"That was the fools in Congress. And the crazy liberals. I

had nothing to do with it." He tried to gauge the Haitian's confused feelings. He must be respectful, but not too respectful, must gradually resume his moral position of strength. Later there would be some way to take his revenge. "So now, maître, you will understand that I must call the Embassy at once. Or Washington if you prefer."

There was a long silence during which he became aware of scratching sounds behind him. This was followed by a clucking that was like a clearing of the throat. It was the white chicken. It had left its roost and begun to circle him. Randall wanted to give it a kick.

At last Hypollite Jasmin made up his mind.

"I will do the telephoning, though not to your filthy Embassy. My aide-de-camp will take you to your quarters. It is not the Ritz, not even the Oloffson. But you will be fed twice a day. The poule will stay with me."

"Telephone any of the newspapers. Telephone the police. You would save time by phoning the Embassy."

"I think I will telephone my dentist Dr. Carlos Monzon." Hypollite Jasmin's lips parted over the horrible teeth, as though to show them off, their quantity of gold. "My dentist is the best dentist in Paris. He knows everything."

An aide-de-camp with a revolver led Randall to the "quarters." They consisted of a large unfinished circular room with stone walls, evidently a tower room, and a small closet into which a portable toilet and wash basin had been installed, unfortunately without running water. Long beams extended across the unlit cavernous attic. One of these served as a walkway between the Assistant Secretary's room and a larger one occupied by an aged black painter named Hauteville. To reach the Assistant Secretary's room it was necessary to enter the painter's apartment by a circular metal staircase and trapdoor, then cross by the walkway.

Three walls of the painter's room were covered with skillful imitations of various nineteenth-century academic painters, also several impressionists. The fourth wall glowed with the yellows and oranges, the loas and serpents and black madonnas of traditional Haitian painting. Randall could tell a Courbet from a Monet, among the imitations, and he could see that all the Haitian paintings were by the same gifted hand. Dimly he recalled being offered a Hauteville painting by one of the dealers in Port-au-Prince. No doubt he was one of those who had been "disappeared."

At the moment the old man was reproducing, apparently from memory, Degas dancers. He looked up from his work in irritation and stared at the intruders. His diabetic eyes bulged. Not much remained of his face except the eyes. The skin was tight over an already discernible skull. He weighed perhaps eighty pounds.

"A revolutionary," the aide-de-camp explained. "He is paying for his communist sins. Also he pays for his bread with paintings which the master sells in Paris."

The painter replied in a querulous high-pitched Creole. Randall understood not a word.

"Speak French, old one. Here is an American to keep you company. He speaks French. Either he is a madman or like you an enemy of the Haitian people. The *maître* has not yet decided which."

Randall told himself the important thing was to keep calm. He tried to assume a manner that had served him well with dignitaries in the steaming Central American capitals. Confidence, friendly tolerance, reserve. A smile that suggested, without giving offence, the enormous power behind him.

"Yes, I will pay. In dollars or French francs as you prefer. The *maître* will see that there has been a misunderstanding. Tomorrow the Embassy could have someone here to pick us up. Even tonight. Anybody who helps me reach the Embassy will be rewarded. You, for instance. How about fifty thousand francs, just to make the call and say where we are? Have you access to the telephone?''

The aide-de-camp laughed.

"The *maître* would kill me.''

"That's true,'' the old painter said. "He would kill you both. I advise you to accept your fate.''

The old painter returned to his Degas dancers.

THE ASSISTANT SECRETARY WAS OBLIGED to sleep on the floor. Only a few rags for a pillow, a mud-caked overcoat for bedding, provided by his fellow prisoner. Early the next morning, however, Gabrielle appeared in the company of a uniformed white French maid carrying a basket of rolls and a pot of coffee. She herself was wearing a lacy summer frock that barely reached her knees. She had washed her hair and doused herself with Shalimar. It was one of his wife's favorites. The familiar scent evoked thoughts of a reunion and the explanations that would have to be made. She would be the more enraged because she had added almost a thousand dollars to the per diem the government would pay for the Meurice suite never slept in.

The French maid looked around the bare attic room in disgust, then at Randall, as though blaming him for the squalor.

"Drink your coffee and eat the bread,'' Gabrielle said. "After that we will descend to the second floor, where you will have a pleasant room, also a bath to be shared with me. I have arranged all that.''

"And your bedroom, who do you share it with to get all these privileges? The 'maître' or one of the assistants?''

For a moment she was irritated, then gave him a friendly smile.

"You are jealous, I think! Are you beginning to like me? You want to keep me for yourself?" She picked up the hand with the bandaged thumb as though for a caress, then changed her mind. "It stinks. I will change the bandage."

"It's infected. I need a doctor to prescribe some antibiotic."

"I will arrange that. First we will go to your comfortable new room."

THERE WERE GRILLS OVER THE the two tall windows. Otherwise the room was pleasant enough, although it would be cold in winter. An immense double bed with high posts sagged in the middle, both armchairs were very worn. On the wall were copies of depressing Utrillos, the grand boulevards in the rain, umbrellas and shiny streets, a winding street in a bleak suburb. But beyond an almost empty moat of greenish scum, the room looked out on rolling hills. Nearby a fine vineyard descended to the village. At the far end of the vineyard two black women wearing white dresses and turbans were at work.

Would his voice calling for help reach the village? That, he quickly decided, would be futile. The Haitians owned the village and everyone in it. His one chance lay in whatever good will Gabrielle could engender in their hosts.

"Sit down, Gabrielle. There. And listen carefully to what I say."

"Yes, monsieur."

"You must persuade the horrible maître that it is in his interest to get us released at once. He will be rewarded, I promise it. If he will even just call the local police . . ."

"He says he will telephone his famous and powerful Paris dentist who will advise him what to do."

"What does a dentist know?"

"Nevertheless that is what he will do. He refuses to call the police."

"Make sure he tells the dentist who I am, my name too, not just my title. And try to get a doctor. Maybe if I'm alone with the doctor for two minutes I could get him to phone the Embassy."

The doctor, however, was one of the Haitians. In Port-au-Prince Randall had attended a simulated voodoo ceremony arranged for tourists. Now he saw at a glance that whatever his medical qualifications, the tall grinning "doctor" carrying a large wicker basket was also a voodoo priest. He introduced himself as Dieudonné Joseph. His worn white robe reached his ankles.

He picked up Randall's hand, sniffed the thumb, twice, and gave off a sound of guttural dismay. Not really a word. He went to the door and shouted out commands in Creole, then opened the wicker basket. First a dirty towel on the floor, then two bottles, one unlabeled, the other rum. Long scissors, a long carving knife, a scalpel with what, unless blood, could only be a streak of rust. Bandage so poorly rolled as to suggest it had been used before. A syringe for injections, placed beside a small and evil-looking bottle. At last a brightly painted gourd attached to a crude handle. In the voodoo ceremony the priest shook just such a gourd over the breasts, stomach and pelvis of a man afflicted with invading hostile spirits.

A woman had stationed herself near the door and was leaning over what appeared to be a steaming brazier. A sickening odor of charcoal had suddenly invaded the room. Two other women in long white dresses and turbans appeared, each with a basin and a moderately clean towel. They could have been the same servants he had seen working in the vineyard a few minutes before. In one of the basins was clean water, in the other what looked like the entrails of a chicken.

Where was Gabrielle? Now that he needed her most she had wandered off.

"I want to see a French doctor," Randall said. "I need pencillin." He repeated the word several times, trying different pronunciations.

"My antibiotic is almost the same," Dieudonné Joseph said. "We brought it from Haiti when the Americans compelled us to leave."

"Please call a French doctor. I will pay you generously to call him."

"My treatment is free."

A bony but remarkably strong hand seized his wrist. With the other hand the priest snipped at the bandage. The Assistant Secretary shrieked.

The thumb was purple with thin streaks of red. The Haitian was appalled.

"Another day and it might have been too late. Excuse me while I roll up your sleeve."

The Assistant Secretary decided the antibiotic was necessary, pencillin or not. He submitted to the baring of his arm and a few dabs of alcohol. The syringe did not look very clean. The needle had certainly been used before. Perhaps often.

"In the name of God put in a new needle."

"I know my business. I have washed this one in hot water and the best alcohol. Haitian rum."

On the third attempt the needle slid under his skin. A

yellow fluid, surely more antibiotic than was necessary, gradually left the syringe and entered him.

At once the room began to recede hazily, the walls were turning into gray shifting sands. As in a dream he heard himself scream.

WHEN HE AWOKE HE WAS IN bed in bright red pyjamas that were much too short. They tore at his crotch.

He had a fresh bandage but his thumb was gone.

Gabrielle was sitting beside the bed, reading. At the sounds of his turning she put down her book and stroked his forehead, gently.

"Don't be concerned, dear one." She said this in a motherly fashion. "What does a thumb matter? Worse things have happened."

Second Sunday

Bargaining

To withhold tactical information that might benefit the perpetrators of this distardly act is one thing. To keep even the appropriate Congressional committees in the dark is another. Must it be left to the free press of two great democracies to suggest that the number of our sworn enemies, from Iran to Cuba, from the FARL of Lebanon to the FMLN of Salvador, is not infinite? This outrage has all the earmarks of a diehard and debilitated communism with its back to the wall. The American people have a right to some kind of statement from the White House.

BUT WHAT WAS THE POOR President to say? One finger pointed east to what was left of Islamic Jihad and Hezbollah, another south to the Sudan, Mozambique, Angola, a third west to

126

the Muslim secessionists in the Philippines. The French looked closer home to Basque separatists and a revived Action Directe and as always to the unreconciled *arabes*. The experts summoned for American talk shows agreed that Central or South American guerillas were the most likely culprits, since the kidnapping had occured on the eve of the Paris conference. The worst and the best had gathered at or near the Lutétia and all the guerilla groups needed cash. In Colombia the leftist guerillas had long depended on the millionaire *narcotraficantes* of Medellín and Cali. But what if those great overlords backed away from their unnatural alliance with revolutionaries? Where then would the guerillas get their money and arms?

A whole week since the disappearance had produced only contradictory statements from Paris and evasion from the White House. The influential dailies and the great weeklies and the talk shows competed for the opinions of retired diplomats and experts on terrorism. There would be competition, in lesser media, for the rumored picture of the Assistant Secretary in the hands (and mouth) of a masked female kidnapper. *Penthouse* might reproduce the original, if it were ever found. But how far would *Playboy* go? In Tokyo an evening tabloid offered, among the usual female breasts and thighs, a cartoon rendering of the alleged event. The White House and State continued to insist that the stories of a compromising FAX were absurd. Even the Washington task force in its secret deliberations had begun to convince itself the picture was a forgery. Randall's wife, however, was contemplating divorce.

In Paris, while CIA, Interpol and Embassy Security stared at their monitors and fingered old files, French agents for the Surveillance du Territoire combed the familiar back streets and dank cellars of petty crime. The page of PARI-

SCOPE opened to advertisements for erotic adventure, the blunder of a FAX sent prematurely, the disappeared femme de chambre Gabrielle and disappeared taxi driver Luc: surely it all added up to an amateurish operation. This meant the Assistant Secretary was doubtless still in Paris, hidden in an attic cubicle or cellar storeroom. The manager of the Sex Shop, interrogated for twenty-four hours straight, in the end babbled nonsense. Meanwhile Gordon Seymour and Pierre Perdoux explored the life of the late François Bouquillon. What, for instance, were his connections with the taxi driver Luc? Where was Luc and where was the femme de chambre Gabrielle Soubiran? Among the many contacts any middle-aged sportswriter would develop, were there any likely to kidnap an Assistant Secretary?

DR. CARLOS MONZON, IN HIS office on the Avenue Montaigne, a quiet Sunday morning, was also raking his memory. Who among the patriots and lovers of order would take physical possession of the Assistant Secretary for a price, and for the sake of real hemispheric solidarity and the restoration of traditional values, not next year or next month but now? And pay a reasonable sum, five million for instance. The colossal blunder with which he had to live—Santander's blunder, his unauthorized transfer of the victims to a barge on the Seine—could blow up in their faces at any moment. For that folly Santander would pay the same price the taxi driver and the sportswriter had paid. The trials of a freedom-loving patriot more than thirty years away from Havana seemed almost too much too bear. How could he give his full attention to a decayed root while his mind followed a decrepit barge along the Loing canal, vulnerable at every lock? He canceled all his appointments.

His mind turned to an immensely rich American widow in her eighties, now living with her two doctors and her several nurses near Marbella. She too was a lover of freedom and had listened entranced to Oliver North. Carlos Monzon knew her mouth well, having traveled twice a year to Marbella to inspect the few real teeth that remained. He had vowed to save them.

She was rich enough to pay the reasonable sum. Unfortunately she lacked discretion. Who knew what story she would pour out on the glorious occasion of the Assistant Secretary's release? Even reveal the exact part played by her beloved and patriotic dentist?

His gloomy reflections were interrupted by Georges Langlade, phoning to inform him of the arrival from Medellín, via Bogotá and Madrid, of Roque Amador Garcia. His private jet, with his famous white Rolls-Royce convertible a fellow passenger. A car known to journalists as *Carro de la Muerte* since it was so often present, with no effort at concealment, near the scene of the bombings. Beside his fortune, the fortune of the decrepit American woman in Marbella was a widow's mite. The *capo* had a suite in the Ritz, two suites in fact, as well as rooms for his considerable retinue. An apartment in Passy was being readied.

"Set up an interview with him, at once. At the Ritz, not in my office."

"It may not be easy getting through to him," Langlade said. "These men are kings."

"Hand deliver a note. Don't telephone. Of course he will see you. Why do you suppose he came to Paris at just this moment? He sniffs an opportunity. Speak to him alone, no names of course. You will say you and I are intermediaries eager for a peaceful solution of the crisis. Tell him we are in touch with people who are in touch with the kidnappers."

"Not I, Carlos. Just you. For me this is the end of the line."

"Don't be silly. There is no end of the line. Just try to set it up for this afternoon. This evening at the latest."

Roque Amador, thirty-four, five-feet-eight, 190 pounds hard as rock, the arms of a wrestler fifty pounds heavier. Marksman, boxer, polo player, billionaire. The *capo* received them in his jockey shorts and a short-sleeved guayabera open over matted hairs. Two young women in the uniforms of nurses, with his initials RAG at the breast pocket, were at work on him, one trimming his toenails, the other massaging his neck and shoulders. They had come with him from Medellín, along with uniformed house servants and secretaries, bodyguards, chauffeur, radio man, lawyer, biographer. And three women friends rumored to be siblings. At the moment the lawyer was conferring with a French associate in a corner of the vestibule, itself a small and elegant salon. There too were managers from the great dressmakers, with assistants carrying samples, and slim-hipped models, both male and female, pacing like restive race horses. The mirrors of the vestibule made last minute primping possible.

The *capo's* green eyes fixed for a moment on Monzon, whom he knew, then questioningly on Langlade, a cold puritanic stare. The eyes suggested some ruthless Anglo ancestor had intervened to modify the burnished complexion and sculptured nose of many generations in Gran Colombia.

Amador waved to a table of delicacies, but with a crispness that encouraged them to refuse. There were lobsters mounted on glowing porcelain, wine in silver coolers, behind the table a grinning uniformed mestizo with a hotel waiter at his elbow. The mestizo was picking at his teeth.

"Sit down there," he said, pointing to a love seat for Monzon and Langlade to share. "So you think my teeth need attention?" He bared them, reaching for the chin of the woman trimming his nails, holding it up firmly. "What do you think of my teeth, *puta*?" he asked, still speaking English.

She shrugged and went back to her work. Beside her was a tray of small silver instruments.

Monzon gestured with an eloquent thumb to the two waiters behind the lobsters, and to a florid young woman who was trying on a dress. But the two nurses would hear every word.

"What I have to say . . ." Monzon began.

"Must be said in confidence?"

A wave of the hand, an expletive Spanish unknown even to Monzon, a playful kick to terminate the pedicure. Playful but it sent the woman sprawling. The four attendants left without delay, also the blonde woman friend tugging at her dress.

"You too," Amador said to Langlade, who jumped up with alacrity. He was glad to leave the room.

They were alone in the gilt and satin room of mirrors worthy of secret negotiations to end a small war in the early years of the century.

"So, Dr. Carlos. What is it you have to tell me?"

"The American fool Randall," Monzon began softly. "You must understand I am acting in a special capacity. An intermediary acting out of good will toward everyone."

"Yes, yes. Where is he?"

"A dentist of my international standing has many connections. Opportunities to be of help. In the present instance I might intervene with patriots wanting the Assistant Secretary in the right hands. Where he might do the most good. I for one am still dedicated to the liberation of my country."

Amador laughed.

"With nothing for yourself? You are trying my patience.

Where is he and how much will it cost me?"

"I don't know exactly."

The *capo* laughed again. Not a pleasant laugh.

"You are lying, Dr. Carlos." He went over to the table and picked up one of the lobsters, tore off a fat claw, then the other. His forearm muscles bulged. He picked up a second lobster and threw it in Monzon's direction. It spattered on the floor. "Try doing that."

The dentist stared at the inert lobster staining the immaculate rose carpet. A small corpse. Perhaps it would have been wiser to go first to the ancient mummy in Marbella. Her hatred of communism might have been worth two million not five, but with far less danger to himself. At least she would not shoot him.

"You are a strong man, Roque. Of Olympic stature, if you put your mind to it. Everyone knows that. Equitation, boxing, polo. Any sport."

"You and I have never really done business, Dr. Carlos. Only the teeth and that only once. I'm not sure you understand me. My ideals, my sacrifices on behalf of the national honor. I think I will show you some family photographs."

He went to the door of the vestibule and shouted a command. Monzon had a glimpse of dismayed models and salesmen waiting. Minutes later a projector and screen were in place.

"I am a rich man, Dr. Carlos. Also a man of culture."

Amador accompanied the slides with a cryptic commentary: *my Ferraris . . . my polo field . . . my sainted mother . . . my Picasso . . . my Tamayo . . . my zoo . . . my island . . . the dean of the university . . . the President . . . the American ambassador . . . my first plane to make deliveries to the Bahamas.* The plane, a two-engine plane of the seventies, hung from the ceiling of an immense living room containing many trophies. In one slide a distinguished visitor was stretched out on a recliner and had removed his dark glasses to look up at the plane.

"The former Minister of Justice. A man with no grasp on realities. He died in an accident."

There was also a slide of a cavernous hall stacked with weapons. A shiny helicopter, rocket launchers, neatly stacked rifles and submachine guns, a small tank, not much bigger in fact than the white Rolls convertible parked on the Place Vendôme.

"The tank is a plaything for my son, who is almost eleven."

A number of pictures showed guests being served luncheon beside a large pool under beach umbrellas. White-jacketed servants hovered in the background, unsmiling and alert. Nude models paraded before the tables, stopping at each to pirouette. The guests, some in bathing suits, some fully clothed, looked on approvingly.

"My annual private competition to select my candidates for Miss Colombia. Notice that the candidates' pubic hair has been shaved. Much neater. I did the shaving myself."

"An excellent idea," Monzon said. "But couldn't we see the pictures on another occasion?"

"You are bored?"

"Of course not."

"I am showing you the pictures because I want you to know me. Some day I will be President of Colombia. Then there will be no unpatriotic extraditions. The sovereignty of our country will be protected. As for the guerillas, there will be no more guerillas. No more communists. No more subversive writers. My ambition is to restore traditional values and a respect for the family."

"That is precisely what I want for Cuba."

The next slides were of military action. A few soldiers in camouflage uniforms on a jungle trail, others standing beside a burning truck. A crashed plane. Army officers with their hands above their heads. Three soldiers hanging from a single branch. A mutilated corpse, the trousers lowered for purposes of exhibition. A crashed plane.

Amador went back to the mutilated corpse.

"This man lied." He looked at Monzon, smiling. "In principle, no one lies to me. I was blamed for this incident."

"I can."

The next picture showed a concrete wall. The palms of two hands, six or seven feet apart, appeared to have been imbedded in the concrete. Above them, rather than below, was a bare foot, the toes pointing up toward the top of the wall. The back of a skull. The gray wall was dusted over with flecks of pebbled black.

"An enemy of the Colombian people," Amador said.

He turned off the projector.

"You look sick, Dr. Carlos. Do you want a drink?"

The dentist did indeed want a drink. He went to the table and poured a glass of white wine, drank it, poured another.

"I understand perfectly the problems of the Colombian people and their oppression by the beasts in Washington. You don't have to tell me."

"The extraditions have to stop," Amador said.

"Of course."

"So where is Randall? The animals in Washington say they won't compromise. But for an Assistant Secretary of State they will compromise."

"I am not exactly sure, Roque, not exactly sure. He fell into the hands of the fool Santander, who turned him over to some Basques for safekeeping. I think I can find him. But they will have to know what you are willing to pay. Five million for example?"

"Dollars?"

"Of course. Say a million on evidence that they have him. The rest on delivery. I will have to turn the details of transfer over to experts."

"I can supply the experts," Amador said. "What evidence have you got?"

"Not I, the Basques. Apparently they have a thumbprint. Also, for confirmation, a small slice of the thumb now kept on ice."

Amador laughed.

"I hope this operation was photographed," he said. "Who did the slicing?"

Dr. Monzon was stunned by the bluntness of the question. He could not think of an appropriate answer.

"What does that matter? The important question is how the transfer is to be managed and where you intend to keep Randall. And the femme de chambre who got the whole thing started. She too must be kept out of the way, Roque. Would you like to have her in your hands?"

"A French woman a candidate for Miss Colombia? Why not?"

So it was imperative to put an end to the comedy of the barge, and to have the Assistant Secretary and the femme de chambre Gabrielle in a safer place. The victims had already left the barge, however, as Monzon learned shortly after returning to his office. The call informing him Randall and Gabrielle had escaped from the barge, only to fall into the hands of his patient Hypollite Jasmin, seemed to Monzon altogether providential. The Assistant Secretary safely in his hands! But before the conversation was over he realized

Jasmin was not going to be cooperative. The man was a fool, one who took no care of his teeth, but he was evidently not ready to surrender his guests on demand.

Jasmin described the Assistant Secretary's hangdog look, his short and oily curled hair, his bandaged thumb.

"No American diplomat would wear his hair in this ridiculous manner," Jasmin said. "The small curls are those of a schoolgirl from the slums. I think this man is an impostor."

"Kidnappers in France have done that before, Hypollite. It is a kind of signature, also it serves to disguise the victim."

They exchanged details on the Assistant Secretary's appearance.

"You have almost convinced me, doctor. I will now call the Grand Patron for advice. I think he would take pleasure in interviewing an American diplomat, even if the diplomat is a madman."

Dr. Monzon was alarmed. Was the Assistant Secretary about to slip out of his fingers, and into those of a more powerful Haitian exile?

"Listen to me carefully, Hypollite. You don't understand the situation. This is an international affair, not something for the likes of you and me. An affair of incalculable consequences. You must get out of this with clean hands, you must be above suspicion, the Grand Patron also. Do you want him thrown out of France?"

"No one will throw him out of France."

"I am in a position to protect you both. I have good friends in the American Embassy. Also at the Quai d'Orsay. The minister himself came to me for an extraction. In the old days they all clamored for American dentists. Now they come to me. In France the condition of the gums is terrible."

There was a long silence.

"I respect you as a dentist," Jasmin said. "But for questions of politics I turn to the Grand Patron. I am a little man."

"Not so little. This could mean a great deal of money. For you alone, Hypollite, not for you to share with the Grand Patron. Listen, my friend, I will come down to La Morinière this evening. We must arrange to do everything with maximum safety for us both. You understand? I can be there by ten o'clock, we can talk face to face. I am only an intermediary but I can guarantee you two hundred thousand dollars, perhaps even three. Just don't do anything until I get there. Keep the man and the girl under surveillance. Locked up, in fact."

"Two hundred thousand dollars! Locked up! Why locked up? You sound like a kidnapper yourself!"

"On the contrary. I am doing my best for everyone concerned. Just obey my instructions and all will be well. I will be there by ten o'clock."

Long before ten, however, the stretch limousine with its dark opaque windows and dimmed lights had left the chateau going south. Gabrielle and Jasmin were in the back seat, a bodyguard who was also the driver in front. Securely locked in the commodious trunk, the well-sedated Assistant Secretary was sleeping comfortably in the fetal position. A small pillow supported his bandaged hand.

Gabrielle

She had often gazed bemused at the long black limousines bringing Meurice guests from the airport, the arriving passengers mysteriously hidden behind dark windows. And now she was gliding through the blue dusk in just such an immense car. The deep leather seats the color of old gold, the armrests wide enough for two, the furry pink slippers the maître Hypollite Jasmin extracted for her comfort from a velvet bag under her seat, the silver embossed compartments behind the driver and the distant glowing dials in front of him, the faint hiss of tires on the asphalt of a country road—all invited her to dream.

Yet it was inappropriate, wrong in fact, for her to be riding in such comfort while the poor Assistant Secretary was locked in the trunk. She intended to rescue him eventually, and deliver him to his friends, especially if she could at the same time save her skin and be assured of a new job. That would take some bargaining. But for the moment she wanted only to free him from the trunk.

"The poor man should be riding with us, maître. I can assure you he will give you no problems. No more than I. He is an intelligent man who accepts reality. Moreover, you can keep a revolver at his ribs."

"Out of the question. Suppose the police were to stop us and turn their powerful lights on the interior? What would they have to say about the revolver?"

"Wouldn't it be worse if they asked to look in the trunk?"

"In that case we would leave without ceremony. This car will go two hundred kilometers an hour. No police could catch us. Moreover, there will be no police. We are following secondary roads. Tomorrow morning the American will wake up under the blue skies of the Côte d'Azur. Cap Ferrat, a paradise. The Grand Patron will give him the treatment he deserves. If he deserves to be released, he will be released. You too, mademoiselle. If there is a reward, you will get your share."

An audacious thought intruded, causing a spasm beneath the ribs. What if she, Gabrielle Soubiran, were to take control of this great car? The largest she had ever driven was a

Peugeot 404. But a car is a car, she would manage. Suppose Hypollite Jasmin decided to relieve himself by the side of the road, modestly, behind a tall hedgerow, and the driver joined him? Men do not like to interrupt that process, there would be a good minute to spare. Would she have the courage to slip to the front seat, turn the key, step on the nearest pedal and thereafter trust to instinct?

She turned to her companion.

"I never dreamed that I, a poor girl from the provinces, would one day ride in such a car. Is it American or French? Is it automatic?"

"German. A Mercedes with many special supplements." Jasmin took a remote control command from the same bag that had produced her slippers, and touched a button. An opaque window slowly rose from behind the front seat, shutting them off from the driver. A succession of buttons, and the four rear windows in turn rose and fell. Still another, and Gabrielle found herself sliding slowly back as in a dentist's chair, while her feet in their pink slippers rose.

"Anything is possible with reclining seats," he said, grinning. She had to look away from the awful teeth. "You would like an aperitif?"

"Yes. But please let me up."

She rose. Another button barely touched, and a small bar swung out from behind the driver. It contained an elegant cut glass service for four: wine glasses of several sizes, two brandy bottles, a bottle of wine in a small silver bucket, a box with plain biscuits, chocolates wrapped in silver foil. A compartment for ice.

She would get them drunk, first the maître, then the driver.

"What is in those bottles?"

He showed her a bottle of Barbancourt rum. It was almost full.

"Not only the best in Haiti. The best in the world. Have a taste."

The rum coursed through her veins. Her plans became more audacious.

"A true Haitian would drink such a bottle in one swallow, no?"

"That is ridiculous. One savors the bouquet, rolls it in the mouth, allow a few drops to be swallowed. This rum is invaluable, a special reserve for the President-for-Life and a few friends. It is one of the treasures we brought with us in the exodus."

"But you are a rich man, maître. Let's see you try."

"Are you hoping to get me drunk, little one?"

"What an idea!"

A touch of the remote control, several clicks, and still another panel at the back of the driver slid away to reveal a small television screen. But the reception was blurred. Many black lines and dots, distant voices.

"Only a refined man of great influence would own such a car, maître. Everything is exquisite." She moved her hand on the armrest, touching his bony black claw. And left her hand there, moving her fingers almost imperceptibly, as though seeking a response from his. Not one of the six zones of pleasure, but a well known preliminary. "I would love to drive this great Mercedes, maître. Do you think I could learn if you were the teacher? Why not now, on this quiet country road?"

"You would kill us in less than five minutes."

"Is it so difficult?"

"Perhaps another time."

"May I try the windows?"

She allowed the black claw to guide her. The window nearest her went down. They were entering the narrow street

of a small village. Old women who were in line at a boulangerie drew back and pressed themselves against the wall.
At the door a young woman her own age looked up from
the racks of bread. Their eyes met. Probably she had never
been to Paris, that girl! Gabrielle, swiftly creating a dream,
saw herself growing up in this gloomy village and meeting
a rich man who stopped to enquire the way to a nearby
chateau. The man would recognize her at once as someone
destined for higher things than a miserable boulangerie. He
would take her to Paris. There she would find a good position
at one of the luxury hotels, the Meurice, for instance.

She lowered the window, raised it, lowered it again. The
village was gone.

"Tell me about your beautiful country, maître. Do you
have postcards?"

"At the Grand Patron's villa you will see slides. The Cathedral, the Presidential Palace, the great hotels. The view
from the heights of Kenscoff."

Conversation was difficult. In addition, she was hungry.
If they were indeed going to the Côte d'Azur by secondary
roads, they would soon be in the zone of the famous small
vineyards and the great restaurants of Burgundy. She had
made two gastronomic tours in the area, once in the company of her communist lover, once with a fat industrial who
always fell asleep after dinner. He would waken her at two
or three in the morning, ready for an exchange of affection.
Ouf!

"Do you know the small towns of Burgundy, maître? You
will find there the best cooking in France. You appreciate
the haute cuisine?"

"We had too much haute cuisine in Talloires. That was
the first refuge in France of the President-for-Life and the
Grand Patron. The natives disliked us."

"We are not far from Joigny, I think. There we had foie gras with green nuts, also coquilles St. Jacques with foie gras. Do you have coquilles St. Jacques in Haiti?"

"We have all seafoods."

"In Avallon we had small ducks with infusion of cassis, in Saulieu we had large ducks with a sauce that included ginger. Extraordinary! Everywhere there are excellent quenelles de brochet. If we take the N6 we will go through both Avallon and Saulieu. I have an idea, maître. Let us stop for the night at the famous Côte d'Or in Saulieu. A comfortable hotel, one of the greatest of restaurants, all in one establishment."

"Where you will doubtless hope to alert the police?"

"If you and I share a room, you could watch over me every minute. Wouldn't you like that? The dinner could be brought to the room."

"I was not born yesterday, little one. You think I'm a fool."

"On the contrary. Listen, maître, I have another idea. You go into the restaurant to order dinner to be brought to the car. I will remain with the driver and the Assistant Secretary in his trunk. Even a simple dinner would be welcome. A jar of foie gras with a loaf of bread and a good wine, that would be enough. Preferably a Chambertin, since we are in the region."

"For the moment you must be satisfied with the biscuits and the chocolates. The best bouchées in Paris. Eat them all if you wish, I am not hungry."

She removed the silver foil from one of the soft nutty chocolates as delicately as she might peel a pear, careful not to smudge her fingers. Enough chocolate nevertheless remained on an index finger to make it worth the sucking. She offered the finger to Hypollite Jasmin. One of the horrible teeth scraped it. Could she go through with her project, even though it might win the Assistant Secretary's gratitude? Not to mention forgiveness and a small reward.

"Not bad," Jasmin said. "If you eat all the chocolates you will not be hungry. At the Grand Patron's villa we will have a Haitian breakfast with a great selection of fruits. Haitian coffee is the best in the world."

She played with the controls. A window slid up and down, the television went on and off, the bar receded into its home. At last she found the control that caused her feet to rise, the rich leather seat to recline.

"I think I will take a nap, maître. Wake me if you change your mind about having a dinner sent out from one of the great restaurants."

She lay back in a luxurious disorientation. What would her lost communist lover think to see her lying thus in the back of a silently gliding Mercedes, with a rising moon curiously transformed by the tinted glass? Soon the maître Hypollite Jasmin was reclining beside her, but as yet had offered no indignities. He was not a great talker, this Haitian, none of the foreigners talked as well as the French! The French also were the best lovers. No, she did not think she could suffer the embraces of Jasmin, that would be too much. But if she could take him up to the moment of truth, and thus have access to his trousers and the keys to the Mercedes while he was in the bathroom, showering, even five minutes in the pleasant shower she would insist he take, and if the stupid bodyguard had also been given a room and the Mercedes waited for her in the moonlit parking lot, with the Assistant Secretary still in the trunk, why then she would simply have to muster her courage and seize the opportunity. How grateful the Assistant Secretary would be when she opened the trunk! Then at last he would know she too was a victim. When all this was over they might take a vacation together, on a cruise for instance, or even on a barge, but this time a tourist barge, not one full of apple brandy.

The man reclining beside her had begun to snore. An odd snore, as though crumpled tinfoil in the throat impeded a rumbling farther down, this followed by a sharp snort, then a whistling as air passed the horrible teeth. The sequence repeated itself many times, but at last began to subside. Her own breathing, delicate and without sound, was also becoming heavier. *Think of pleasant experiences*, she admonished herself, hoping to induce an agreeable dream. To glide for instance on a luxurious barge on the Canal du Midi, not the Canal du Loing, with the Assistant Secretary beside her in a white suit, now shaved and his hair grown back to a reasonable length and its true color restored. They would have dinner on the deck, a linen tablecloth engraved with her initials, a pungent cassoulet of the region and the best St. Emilion served by a young black servant whose teeth were flawless and whose skin under his tunic would be as soft as the flesh of a peeled pear. She and the Assistant Secretary, whose thumb was apparently growing back: surely they deserved a quiet vacation after so many weeks, even months of discomfort and anxiety.

The barge on the Canal du Midi was slowing to less than the pace of a peasant walking on the towpath. Moments before there had been no peasant; now there he was, waving to her in a friendly fashion. Not a bad looking man, to tell the truth. She was pleased to observe that he was walking in time with her own ever deeper breathing, the right foot advancing slowly, the left then forcefully stepping ahead. She understood now why the peasant was walking so slowly, the barge was about to enter a lock. She could hear rushing waters. The gates opened wide.

The peasant had vanished, his blue smock was gray and

translucent, he had disappeared without waving goodbye. And the barge had translated itself into a great car, the Mercedes in fact, which was silently gliding on a country road. She knew that road, she knew those vineyards on their moonlit slopes. How far they had come! Avallon and Saulieu were already behind them, they had just passed Chagny, where she had enjoyed a remarkable dish composed of the tails of shrimp in many sauces, she and her communist lover. Extraordinary shrimp that swimming in their sauce appeared to be alive. The thick white tails freed of their carapace bubbled and pulsed in an amusing, even alarming manner. The legs of frogs, it was well known, continued to kick after death. That was Chagny, where the tall chef insisted on standing beside their table, holding a living frog for their inspection as another chef might display a lobster. But Chagny too was gone, soon they would be in Chalons, where she had once seen the Saône in flood. It was there they would join the high speed autoroute for an uninterrupted journey to the Côte d'Azur.

Perhaps the maître Hypollite Jasmin knew it must be now or never, if he was to enjoy her favors. She could feel his desire in the dark, knew his hand wanted to touch hers. Slowly she slid her hand across the wide armrest until it reached his bony claw. A skeletal claw, as though all the flesh were gone. Would she dare to renew her suggestion, even invitingly touch the lobe of a wrinkled ear? She shuddered. Breathing deeply, she returned to the Canal du Midi and its barge, with the Assistant Secretary beside her.

But it now appeared her gentle touch had aroused the maître's interest. It was he not the Assistant Secretary beside her. The silent car was slowing, the maître had already given the command in those Haitian tones that sounded like a grieved lover's accusation. A glowing sign: the AUBERGE DE

L'ESPERANCE. Evidently the maître must have felt the small and isolated auberge, only a miserable huddle of cinderblock cabins, offered no menace. They stopped. The proprietor, who had given up hope of customers, met them in his pyjamas. Drooping pyjama trousers, the blouse open over gray hairs. But no, he was wearing no blouse, the moonlight shone on his fat belly. There were no other cars next the row of dark cabins that led away from the road into a thick grove of trees. The last cabins were hidden, and the maître was inspecting one of these. Evidently the proprietor was too tired to accompany him, even though they were the only customers. But already Jasmin was returning to tell her that the cabin would be satisfactory. Theirs was the last in the row, at the edge of a wilderness. But for the moment it would have to do.

"To begin with, there is no telephone. So much the better! Also no luxury. A shower, but no bath. Tomorrow in the villa of the Grand Patron you will have a chance to enjoy the luxuries, you and the Assistant Secretary."

"Please let him out, maître. At least let him stretch his legs."

"He is asleep. He will be tranquilized for ten hours more. At least."

"May I look?

They opened the trunk. The Assistant Secretary did indeed appear to be sleeping peacefully. His breathing was like that of a healthy adolescent boy, one whose skin was soft and white. The trunk light cast a pleasing glow over his features. She felt a rush of motherly affection for the sleeping man, and ran her fingers through his stiff curls. How he had changed in the few days of their relationship! How much gentler he had become! The stiff curls were, however, unpleasantly oily. At the first opportunity she would personally administer a good shampoo.

They closed the trunk softly.

"You are a cultured and compassionate man, maître. I hope you will let the poor driver have a room for a few hours' sleep."

"What a ridiculous idea. He guards the car. If he were to fall asleep, that would be his last sleep."

She tried to conceal her disappointment. It now appeared her ingenious plan was doomed, even if she were to gain access to the trousers.

They walked along the dark cabins to the one they had been assigned, apparently the only one ready for occupancy. Ahead was the dark forest. The maître preceded her, striking away tall weeds that impeded their progress. The poorly furnished cabin was cold even on this summer night. The only window was broken, a spider had spun its web across the vacant space. One straight chair, no armoire or closet, a lumpy double bed with a patched coverlet. No television. The bed sank in the middle, as though generations of sleepers had huddled there for warmth. Even in the arms of her communist lover she would have detested such a bed.

"It is not the Meurice, maître. But at least there are modern facilities. You must take a long shower. Five minutes at least."

Jasmin inspected the bathroom. A spitting sound, then an uneven rush of water.

"There is only one spigot for the basin. Probably no hot water. Besides, I don't need a shower."

"In everything else you give the commands, maître. In the affairs of the heart it is the woman."

She was astonished by her own audacity. But he assented

with only a bit of grumbling and was soon down to disagreeable shorts that reached the knobby knees. He modestly withdrew to the bathroom. Fortunately his bowels had stirred, he had seated himself, this would give her time. No need to wait for the shower. But no, he was already in the shower. She explored his trousers pockets quickly, attentive to the uneven flow of water from the bathroom. Sometimes a rush, sometimes little more than a trickle. There was nothing of interest in his pockets. The stub of a pencil, a soiled handkerchief, a smooth chestnut, a stick of gum, a few coins, no keys. The handkerchief decided her. She was simply incapable of making love with the maître Hypollite Jasmin.

She quietly took the long room key out of the door, left the room, and locked it from the outside. On the way to the car she would think of something.

She was surprised to see that the massive hood of the car had been raised. The driver was leaning over the engine, examining it with a flashlight. Was he listening for an irregular sound? The engine was running!

He looked up, turned the flashlight on her, then on her hand holding the long door key. No response. The light returned to her face, searched her eyes. She was afraid that powerful light would penetrate her intention.

"What are you doing? What do you want?"

"Help!" she gasped. "It is the maître."

"What is it with the maître?"

"He is dying. He had a heart attack while taking a shower. Hurry! I will telephone for a doctor."

The driver stared. He was very tall, much taller than she had realized. His skin in the thin light seemed gray rather than black, a transparent gray, in fact. He looked like one of those Haitians who rise from the dead. Would he in his panic leave the engine running? He did.

She waited until he had disappeared down the corridor of dark cabins.

She prayed.

Without lowering the hood she got into the driver's seat and reached with her foot for the accelerator, touched it as softly as one might touch a lover's or child's wrist. Nothing, only a cat's purr. But of course! She must put the car in *drive*. Or, if that's the way things turned out, in *reverse*. It was impossible to see in this darkness.

The car shot back and struck a post. She tried another gear and it leaped forward, knocking over and crushing a bicycle stationed where no bicycle should be. No time now to get out and lower the hood. The car careened to the left and struck the side of a barn. A terrible splintering, a side of the barn was about to fall. Dismayed, she leaned out the door to see where she was going. A miracle! The great car, ignoring her commands, had righted itself and was already back on the narrow moonlit road. So now, not now but soon, she could stop to lower the hood, then drive on. In the still night she heard the ghostly wail of a far-off train. It was like the swooning drawn-out cry of a lost soul dissolving in the night. Or could it be, far behind her, the shrieks of the Haitian driver?

No matter. Another few kilometers and she would turn onto a side road, open the trunk and wake the Assistant Secretary. He would be too heavy for her to carry.

The Mercedes moved under her hands in silent obedience, as though she had been driving such a car all her life. But where was she going? Once on the autoroute A6, where in fact she already was, it would be difficult to turn back north. She could instead continue on beyond Lyon to the Restaurant Pyramide in Vienne, where the patronne would surely remember her. A memorable thrush paté, with an actual stuffed bird on a branch! A crimson lobster and golden duck! How could the restaurant forget her industrial's monumental tip? There was a decent small hotel nearby. But wouldn't it be splendid, a success never to be forgotten, to turn around and return by back roads to Paris, to the Meurice in fact, and in the early hours of the morning find her way to the rue Mont Thabor and glide under the hotel's great porte-cochère, even alert the sleepy doorman with a sharp blow on the horn? *"Here is the missing American diplomat. Please help him to his old apartment."*

But oddly enough this great moment too was already in the past, although she was still driving south, with Lyon behind her not ahead. Already the Assistant Secretary had been released to rejoin his unattractive wife in Washington. No, that unfortunate event was still in the future. For the great Mercedes was continuing on its effortless way to the Côte d'Azur, virtually without her guidance, even to Marseille and the Cannebière, where her communist lover had gone to live, then on to St. Tropez, Cannes, Nice, the Hotel de Paris in Monte Carlo.

There under a blazing sun she stood near the entrance to the gaming rooms, waiting to be photographed, first in a swimsuit of an earlier and more romantic era, with one hand on the door to the driver's seat, then in a short white skirt for tennis, a racket over her shoulder, at last in a black evening gown ruffled provocatively over both abdomen and buttocks, with the graceful back entirely bare...

Alas, it was not to be exactly like that. It was a dream, all a dream, there was no cabin at the edge of a wilderness, no Auberge de l'Espérance. She woke to the broad daylight of the Côte d'Azur, yes, but with Hypollite Jasmin beside her. Nice was already behind them, they had passed Cannes while she slept. Moments later they stopped at the high gates of the Villa Bon Aventure on Cap Ferrat.

Two guards with submachine guns were peering in on them, one on each side of the car.

monday

The Grand Patron

THE ASSISTANT SECRETARY AWOKE TO immaculate white walls and a French window thrown open to a wide balcony and to sunlight and blue sky. His white pyjamas were of gossamer silk, so too the sheets of the vast double bed. The mattress was at once firm and sensuously resilient, delicate fingertips rippled beneath its silken cover. The bandaged thumb still dully ached and throbbed, but his body felt warm and cleansed as after a long massage and bath. A scent of Shalimar seemed to emanate from himself. Touching his face, he discovered that someone had shaved him while he slept.

He knew at a glance that he was no longer in La Morinière. Here he was, wherever that was, as helpless as a child. But for the moment he felt no anger. The chain and the whip

152

of the aged Santander, the fellation while he slept, the slice of thumb lost and eventually the whole thumb . . . And now to wake in an unknown place in exquisitely soft pyjamas not his own. It all left him with a sense, not entirely unpleasant, that he was no longer master of his destiny and that a subtle change in his character had occurred.

And now to find someone had shaved him while he slept! Where was Gabrielle?

She was in the doorway, smiling. She too was in white silk pyjamas. The letters GP were sewn above a small pocket over one breast. Over the other was an embroidered Haitian flag. He touched his own pyjamas. They were decorated in the same way. A glance at the other pillow told him Gabrielle had lain beside him.

"You have slept for eighteen hours, monsieur. Now you will feel like a new man."

"Someone shaved me."

"One of the nuns shaved you, another bathed you all over, I supervised. The women servants here are called nuns, but they are not really nuns." She sat down on the side of the bed and touched his cheek. Would she dare to stroke it? "This is the most wonderful place, monsieur. Everything is in the best taste. There is a salon with many books, another with many paintings. In some respects this villa is more remarkable than the Hotel Meurice. Only a man of culture could inhabit it."

"You've seen the Grand Patron?"

"Only for a moment."

"Will he listen to reason?"

She frowned.

"Why be in a hurry? Let us first enjoy this luxury. Our Haitian breakfast will arrive at any moment."

And here it was. Three young black maids in all but transparent Empire gowns of white muslin appeared at the door, smiling. Behind them were serving carts with silver tureens and cut glass decanters. The women were at once provocative and innocent, as though unaware of their bodies moving sensually under the muslin. They curtsied and chirped greetings.

"These are the nuns," Gabrielle said. "They will serve us breakfast on our balcony."

The table had been laid while he slept. A linen tablecloth with the GP and embroidered Haitian flag. Gardenias floated in a silver dish. Bowls of fruit appeared, each nun carrying one. Glowing pomegranates among russet pears and purple plums, peaches worthy of Cézanne. Melons sliced in the shape of scimitars. Cut glass goblets of orange juice. A champagne bottle in its silver bucket of ice. Even the bucket had the insignia GP. Glasses for the champagne.

The balcony overlooked terraced gardens and a hillside of olive trees sloping steeply to the bay of Villefranche. The Assistant Secretary had been on Cap Ferrat before. He knew where he was, he knew it was the bay of Villefranche. At the moment they were standing on the crest of the cape's divide. To the east was a deep bowl of calm water, long a home for ships of the American navy, the bay ending at the steep-terraced town of Villefranche-sur-Mer. From the other end of the balcony he could see, far below, the smaller Baie des Fourmis and the villas and white hotels of Beaulieu-sur-Mer. In the blue distance were Cap Martin, Monaco, Italy.

The thin drone of a speedboat pulling a water skier rose from the bay of Villefranche. A destroyer, small as a child's toy, was anchored a few hundred yards from the town's quay.

Directly beneath the balcony black servants were cleaning the tables and beach umbrellas around a long pool. A bank of carnations sloped gently down to formal privet hedges where several gardeners were at work clipping. Beyond was a dense encircling hedge gone wild. But no signs of armed guards.

What would happen if he shouted for help at the top of his voice? Nothing, presumably. Would the servants and gardeners even look up?

The nuns reappeared with more dishes. An omelet of shredded herbs crossed with strips of red pepper, bordered by mussels in their shells. A basket of croissants and brioches, butter shaped in the semblance of roses, jams in silver pots. Coffee that gave off a faint odor of charcoal and chicory when the silver lid was lifted.

The three nuns hovered at the end of the balcony, smiling. Gabrielle reached for the Assistant Secretary's right hand and covered his four remaining fingers.

"If I were rich I would want to buy this place."

An engraved card arrived, with a handwritten message: the Grand Patron wished to pay his respects. No name on the card, only the now familiar GP and Haitian flag. And here he was, tiptoeing toward them: a small emaciated mulatto, ageless and pockmarked but with thin lips and a fine straight nose. He was wearing a spotless Panama hat and white kid gloves. He kissed Gabrielle's hand, bowing with the ease of a dancer. And touched the Assistant Secretary's wrist, gently, as to commiserate on the lost thumb.

The Assistant Secretary had an uneasy feeling that he had met this man before. The white gloves, the gray buttons covering the face. Was that a copy of *Figaro* sticking out of his hip pocket? How could he get his hands on it?

"I appreciate the honor of having you as my guest." The voice was sinuous, cultured, ingratiating. "I will do everything to make you comfortable."

The Assistant Secretary felt his rage returning. How much of this comedy would he have to put up with? He became aware that two young persons were watching sullenly from the doorway, as though they had been commanded to appear. At a wave of a kid glove they approached. The boy was fourteen or so, slim and with a languid elegance, wearing only tennis shorts. The girl was perhaps a year younger. Both were barefoot. The boy was of a light coffee color. The girl's face was bronzed from the sun, but her long legs were almost white. She too was wearing shorts but also a loose blouse that had not been buttoned.

The Assistant Secretary had a startling glimpse of a firm small breast surmounted by a dark and surprisingly large nipple.

"These are my dear friends Ti Roro and La Séductrice. You may say anything in their presence."

He took off the gloves slowly, as though to call attention to the emerging fingers, which were long and thin. The nails had been painted orange. The boy and the girl looked at each other and grinned.

"Your friends, monsieur?" Gabrielle asked. "Surely you mean your children. They are so beautiful!"

"Orphans. I saved them at the time of the exodus. Haitian women are famous for their beauty, but the beauty of the men must not be overlooked. Look at Ti Roro's skin! Stroke it as you would a statue. Come here, Ti Roro, and let the American stroke your skin."

The boy stuck out his tongue, not smiling. He helped himself to one of the pears, examined it, then handed another to the girl. They drifted off to the end of the balcony with the indifference of rich children. Their curiosity had been satisfied. They stood close together, looking down at the pool.

The three nuns watched from the other end of the balcony.

"Please continue with your breakfast," the Grand Patron said. "If you permit I will join you."

A wave of his long fingers, two of them extended, had an instant response. One of the maids rushed to bring up a chair. The others trotted out of the room, and returned almost immediately with a place setting for the master.

"The nuns also are beautiful," Gabrielle said. "Everything here is beautiful."

"They too were rescued."

The Grand Patron was toying with one of the gloves, as though debating whether to put it back on. Yes, the Assistant Secretary was convinced he had met this pockmarked wraith at the time of the negotiations. A man resembling him sat a few feet behind the President-for-Life, putting on and taking off gloves. As the Grand Patron was doing now.

"Why don't you tell me what you want?"

"I want to protect you, Mr. Secretary. You have had bad luck. More bad luck might follow. I appreciate the wisdom of my friend Hypollite Jasmin in bringing you here, though he made the mistake of consulting a dentist in Paris. In La Morinière your enemies might have found you. Here you are among friends."

He took the newspaper out of his pocket and laid it on the table, but folded. Reading upside down, the Assistant Secretary looked for his name. Only a plane crash in Canada. Hundreds dead.

"What enemies?"

"The PLO for one, but also all communists. Your State Department refuses to affirm or deny it is in contact with the PLO." He tapped the newspaper on the table. "How would you like to be a guest of the PLO, Mr. Randall? Sheep's eyes or sheep's balls for breakfast, not this delicious Haitian omelet. Does this story mean the PLO had you imprisoned on that barge? Luckily you escaped and now you are here where I can protect you." He nodded to the untouched omelet. "You are not doing justice to your breakfast."

The Assistant Secretary took a small fiery taste of the omelet. He picked up the newspaper. Only a small double-column story at the bottom of the first page! FURTHER WHITE HOUSE DENIALS. At the Department briefing a statement from the French Ministry of the Interior was read. It urged patience. Every avenue was being explored. A roundup of terrorists was continuing. If secret meetings were occuring they would not be announced. If announced they would cease to be secret.

"Yes, of course, you are 'protecting me'. Now if you want to protect yourself, monsieur . . ."

"My first name is Toussaint, after the heroic general, my last name is Bazile. Among my ancestors was the great Dessalines. You may use the first name or the last, not both together."

"Thanks. Now as for my enemies . . ."

"They are numerous. Think of how many would pay to have you in their hands! The communists, who would tear you limb from limb and broil you on spits. But also the loyal enemies of communism betrayed by the U.S. Betrayed even by you personally, Mr. Randall. For thirty years in Haiti the father and then the son held your communist enemies at bay. Jean-Claudisme protected order in the Caribbean. It beat off the crazy guerillas. The President-for-Life was your friend. And then you lost your nerve, the Secretary of State also lost his nerve. And you were there! I saw you, Mr. Randall. You were there when the President-for-Life made his sacrifice. Even you are a paragraph in the long tragic history of Haiti."

"I was the one betrayed, monsieur. Monsieur Toussaint. My motives were misunderstood. But let's talk business, not politics. What can you possibly hope to get out of holding me?"

"Only justice, Mr. Secretary. Only restoration of what was deceptively taken from us at the time of the disorders and the exodus. My hotel, my share of the National Lottery, my art gallery in Pétionville, my villa. All that is but a bagatelle, I speak only for myself, the Grand Patron. Consider the dishonor for the President-for-Life, not to mention his holdings in New York, Miami and Port-au-Prince. The dishonor has no price."

"So you think the United States government will get your art gallery back? Or a bit of the National Lottery?"

"At least you can get us all admitted to the United States where our compatriots in New York are waiting to honor us."

An awkward silence. Gabrielle broke it. She was not in the habit of keeping still so long.

"That is not too much to demand, to be admitted to the United States. I too would like that. Surely you can arrange it."

The Assistant Secretary laughed.

"Wait till we've finished breakfast. Then I'll call the President."

"You are joking, monsieur. You are once again making fun of me."

He felt a stir of affection, even wanted to touch her hand.

"Just a poor girl from the provinces," he said gently.

"She is a sweet innocent," the Grand Patron said, as though he had known her for years and was delivering a benediction. "But let us face reality. You have many enemies. Do you know a Dr. Carlos Monzon, the Paris dentist?"

"No."

"I have on good authority that he is interested in your person, not only your teeth. Beware of him. But the worst are the *traficante* animals from Colombia. One has arrived in Paris. I assure you I will do what I can to protect you from them. And protect your innocent friend. She tells me she too is a victim." He began to peel off the gloves again. "But you must cooperate."

THE POWERFUL SEDATION ADMINISTERED IN La Morinière might have dissolved his will to rise; he slept again. When he awoke it was early afternoon, and heat was pouring into the room. It even seemed to have settled on his forehead like a hot hand. Sun burned on the balcony railing, the white walls glared. The hand on his forehead was, in fact, Gabrielle's. She was looking down on him solicitously, as to assess a possible fever. He found himself staring at two small but splendid bare breasts only inches from his mouth. The silken kimona had fallen open as she leaned above him, and she was wearing, otherwise, only a striped black and orange bikini. In the hand not stroking his forehead were men's swim trunks, white except for the letters GP.

"You must get up, monsieur. A swim in the pool will renew your energies."

"I can't swim with this bandage on."

"You can walk about in the water to refresh yourself. I will walk with you. After that you can have your Haitian cocktail and lunch beside the pool and watch us swim."

"Us?"

"Ti Roro and La Séductrice do a splendid dance of water serpents, swimming under the water. They have offered to teach me."

She pulled the sheet away, leaving him quite naked. His still slumbering penis stirred briefly, then fell back.

"Oh la! You are reviving at last! Would you like me to help you, monsieur?"

The compromising photograph intruded at a corner of his mind. He wished it away.

"Help me?"

"With the bathing suit."

"I can manage by myself."

Several tables had been set by the pool, as though guests were expected, but only the Grand Patron was there, fully dressed, with a bottle of champagne cooling beside him. The *Figaro* was next to his glass. A nun was in attendance with towels, two waiters in white jackets hovered near a table with silver dishes and an array of bottles. One of the waiters was white, probably a Frenchman. Could the white waiter be bribed to take a message to the outside world?

Ti Roro and La Séductrice were paddling lazily near the diving board. They were swimming nude. The water glittered, the Assistant Secretary's eyes burned in the sun.

They sat down beside the Grand Patron, who insisted on shaking hands.

"Will you join me in champagne? A fruit punch with Haitian rum? Your American bourbon? Malt Liquor from Scotland? Stolnichaya?"

How much, exactly, did this zombie know? What had Hypollite Jasmin told him?

"How about apple brandy? Calvados."

The Grand Patron laughed.

"You are thinking of your misadventure on the barge! I will tell you something you perhaps don't know. Your kidnappers nearly drowned in brandy escaping from one of the tanks."

"How could that be?" Gabrielle said.

"It is here in the newspaper, an amusing *fait divers* on a back page. Someone locked them in. Was it you, mademoiselle? Or you, Mr. Randall? The miserable ones tried to get out through one of the tanks. But the tank was not empty. It spilled out on them. They almost drowned! And do you know what the Basque sailors called you? 'An American criminal and his girlfriend who had taken over the barge at gunpoint.' "

Who then were the kidnappers? What else did they tell the police? The Assistant Secretary scanned the little story. They were *Basque sailors taking brandy to Burgundy*. That was all.

"You must know more, monsieur Toussaint. What did Jasmin tell you?"

The Grand Patron waved two fingers. The French waiter filled their glasses.

"Hypollite Jasmin has a theory, but his theories are always wrong."

"Colombians? Iran? PLO? I can't believe it was only Basque separatists behind them."

"I don't know any more. You stumbled into La Morinière, Mr. Secretary, you and your beautiful innocent. That was pure chance, a Haitian fatality. Until Jasmin called you had scarcely entered my thoughts. How could I hope you would fall into our hands? Instead I imagined you in the hands of the Libyans, undergoing the worst tortures. They would have skinned you alive to obtain the names of the CIA's. So far you have lost only a thumb."

"Where is Jasmin now?"

"He is for the moment indisposed." He clapped his hands sharply, looking at the idling swimmers. "Now it is time for the ballet. You will see a Haitian dance of the siren and the serpent. To work, Ti Roro! Go to it, La Séductrice!"

"I'm tired," the boy said.

"Me too."

The Grand Patron clapped his hands more imperiously. At once the two began to swim toward the center of the pool. They advanced in long languid side strokes, facing each other a few feet apart, then broke away to begin a leisurely yet wary circling, nude wrestlers on the alert for an opening, hands extended, coming together for a moment's touch only to glide away. La Séductrice rolled, scissoring, a slow roll of white buttocks and dark pubis and white buttocks again, a sporting fish while the boy Ti Roro circled watching, then lay on his back to float, the brown appendage now growing from his loins, brown then blue in the water then gone as he turned away. The boy gasped, took a long breath, and dove. La Séductrice followed him, diving. They came up for breath and swam closer to the spectators and dove again. Now they could be seen more clearly, Ti Roro approaching, his blue penis ripplingly distended, she no siren now, offering herself with legs apart, arms flailing to keep up. Another break of the surface for breath, another dive, their blue bodies now inches apart. The Grand Patron stood up. He took off his gloves and began to clap his hands, sharply, in time with the writhing bodies. The two bodies now under water came together as one.

A long embrace. They came to the surface, gasping.

"A Haitian story," the Grand Patron said. "It can also be celebrated in bed."

"It's amusing, don't you think? The children have invited me to join." Gabrielle glanced at his bandaged hand. "Would you like to participate?"

The Grand Patron appraised her.

"It can be celebrated with two serpents and one siren. Or

three serpents and two sirens. Any combination is possible."

An unpleasant image of his office in Washington intruded with an hallucinatory clarity. His wife was there, sitting on his desk. They were looking at photographs, she and his puritanic superior, the Secretary of State. The Secretary himself, also sitting on his desk!

"I can imagine," the Assistant Secretary said.

"It might be amusing," Gabrielle said. "In the pool, I mean, all of us in the pool. Would you like to try, monsieur? You can hold your hand above the water."

"Another time," he said, thinking of the two on his desk in Washington.

HE SLEPT AGAIN. AT DINNER the Grand Patron brought up again the name of Dr. Monzon, who had urged Hypollite Jasmin to turn his guests over to him. Their table was on a terrace overlooking the bay of Villefranche. It was still not fully dark, but a few lights already dotted the hillside. Nuns hovered, a waiter stood ready to pour wine.

"This dentist has many patients among the Americans of Paris. Not only Paris, he has even treated one of my neighbors. A rich American lady, a fanatic who has lost her wits. Dr. Monzon is a Cuban exile, a dedicated foe of the communists. So much to the good, I too am a dedicated foe of the communists. However, this dentist was determined to get you and he had no intention of returning you to the American Embassy. He offered Jasmin two hundred thousand dollars for your person. Why would he do that if his purposes were pure?"

"Like your own purposes?"

"I was defrauded, the President-for-Life was defrauded. We had every democratic right to expect your support against the anarchic rabble. If Dr. Monzon was defrauded it was centuries ago when his men were left by the CIA to die on the beach at the Bay of Pigs. There is no comparison between me and the Cuban dentist.''

"I won't argue with you about that. I won't go into Department politics either. But why are you telling me about Monzon?''

"It will be necessary to take precautions if the dentist turns up here, which I find very likely. Unpleasant precautions.''

"Like turning us over to the President-for-Life for a little Jean-Claudisme?''

"Of course not. The President-for-Life remains in the realm of ideas. He is planning for our return to democracy. He has novel ideas for elections. The President-for-Life hates violence, it is a fact not everyone knows.''

"That's true, not everyone knows it.''

Three lobsters arrived, cold, on beds of ice. The meat had been arranged around the tails, with flowerets of mayonnaise under the claws.

"I don't want you to fall into the dentist's hands. So far you have lost only a thumb. But if the hand were to become infected I could always call on a reliable surgeon in Beaulieu for a necessary amputation. A man who asks no questions.''

The Assistant Secretary pushed his dish away.

"I'm not going to listen to threats. Tell me exactly what you want.''

"I want you to make a video cassette to be sent to Paris, also a copy to Washington. In it you can give your personal recommendations. We don't ask for concessions, we don't ask for the release of prisoners. A little money, of course, a little money as a matter of principle, one or two million. But the main thing is to have us admitted to the United States. Only twenty good citizens, freedom fighters, lovers of order and democracy. Only twenty. We will have to leave a few nuns behind."

"The immigration service would laugh at you. And at me."

"That would depend on the cassette. Let's be reasonable. What would a few more Haitians matter, not more than twenty, when there are already so many thousands?"

Later, over coffee, the talk of "protection" resumed.

"And how would you protect us? With the nuns? This place is totally vulnerable."

"You think so? Let me take you on a little tour of the Villa Bon Aventure. Or you can simply stay here and watch." He took a small black box out of his breast pocket, thinner than a telecommand for remote control. "Come to the edge of the terrace."

Underwater lighting gave the pool a blue phosphoresent glow. Beyond it, the carnation bed and privet hedges descended into a gathering darkness. The Grand Patron held up the box for them to see. At a touch several rows of opal white buttons lit up. He pressed one of the buttons. Instantly the grounds were flooded with light. Even individual branches were outlined in the curving wilderness at the bottom of the estate more than a hundred yards below the house.

"A splendid French creation. The Japanese are not the only ones with brains."

"That is true," Gabrielle said. "A Frenchman invented the movies. I forget his name. Also there was Madame Curie. The Paris subway is the best in the world."

The Grand Patron touched a second button and a screeching alarm was succeeded by a wailing siren. A touch of the same button and the siren ceased. A third button, and a number of men in camouflage uniforms stepped from the trees. At least fifteen men, emerging from different parts of the curving wilderness. They were carrying submachine guns. Most of them were barefoot.

"Very impressive," the Assistant Secretary said. "You've made your point."

"I don't like that sort of thing," Gabrielle said.

The Grand Patron held the box close to his mouth, whispering. The command echoed stridently from loudspeakers behind them in the house and from different parts of the grounds. The exercise was over. The uniformed men retreated into the thick vegetation. The floodlights went out.

"I want to go back to Paris," Gabrielle said.

"Don't worry, little innocent. I, Grand Patron, will personally take care of you. I will now show the place where you will be perfectly safe, even if evil dentists want to seize you."

He led them to a large room with many Haitian paintings. One of the largest paintings, *Le Paradis Terrestre*, began almost at the floor and was more than six feet high. Adam and Eve, mulattos, reclined under a tree of purple fruit while benevolent lions and curious giraffes watched.

Their guide took out the black box again, pressed a button, and the painting moved. It became a door. Behind it a narrow stone stairway descended to the cellar. A cold dank breath of stale air.

In the cellar were four barred cells feebly lit from ceiling bulbs.

The first two contained stacked arms. Assault rifles, submachine guns, grenades. In the third two black women in the muslin nun's costumes were huddled on a bench at the back of the cell. Metal dishes as for a dog were on the floor, water had spilled from one of them. The Grand Patron greeted the women in dialect. He did not sound unfriendly.

"These nuns were insubordinate. They thought they had

to work too hard. I never ask the nuns to work too hard."

They moved to the fourth cell. A tall black man, naked, stood with his hands holding the bars defiantly. Even in the faint light it was possible to see his terrible teeth. The Assistant Secretary knew those teeth.

It was Hypollite Jasmin.

"But that is the maître!" Gabrielle said. "Why is he in this cell, and why is he nude?"

"He too was insubordinate. He made the mistake of consulting Dr. Monzon before calling me."

"Only for information, Grand Patron," Jasmin pleaded, "only for information."

"The mistake could be a very expensive one. Consider your problems if this dentist comes to Villa Bon Aventure? My secretary is calling all the hotels, I would not be surprised if Monzon is already in Nice. You have lost a thumb, Mr. Randall. Would you also want to lose a few teeth?"

"You must do what the Grand Patron wants," Gabrielle said. "What harm is there in a video cassette?"

AND AGAIN THE ASSISTANT SECRETARY slept. Would he spend the rest of his life sleeping? He woke to the sound of a wailing accordion and the husky lament of an Edith Piaf recording. It came from some distant part of the house. A sickle of moon hung at an upper corner of the French window thrown open on the warm night. Gabrielle was sitting on the side of the bed. She was wearing only a loose kimono, which was open over her breasts, shadowed and blue but with a faint perfumed sheen. He now saw what had wakened him, the touch on his ankles and chest and navel of a bundle of feathers attached to a stick. He had managed to put on the pyjamas trousers, but apparently had been too tired to remove his socks. She continued to tickle him.

"I went to the bathroom and when I came back you were already asleep. Is it the pills you take three times a day after the operation on the barge? You have been asleep a whole hour. I think you sleep too much. It is not healthy to sleep so much."

"An hour! Where have you been?"

She touched an ear lobe with the feathers, first the left ear, then the right.

"I was bored so I visited with Ti Roro and La Séductrice. We were listening to the music."

"In bed, no doubt."

She laughed. She touched his nipples with the feathers, circling first the left nipple then the right.

"For the zone of pleasure it is better with a finger dipped in brandy."

"Did the Grand Patron join in the fun? Or just watch?"

"The Grand Patron has gone away in his big car to Nice. He is making enquiries about the dentist Dr. Monzon. So the young people are free to do what they want." She tickled his navel gently. "They invite you to join them to listen to the good music and to play games. The games are optional."

"And who will take the pictures this time?"

She brushed his legs with the feathers, through the pyjamas, first the left leg then the right. The feathers rested momentarily on his loins.

"That was Luc's idea. Not my idea at all. In time you will forgive me."

Absurdly, he wanted to say he had forgiven her, who at the least might well have ruined his career. For the moment his office seemed very far away. The Secretary of State was sitting on the desk. His wife had gone home. His office was a mess.

"Permit me," she said. She took the lobe of his right ear in her mouth and sucked it. "I would have agreed to a photograph of that, only the ear, nothing more than that." She stroked the left ear while continuing to suck the right. "If you want me to stop I will stop. I will leave you and go back to my young friends. They too are victims, in a way, even though the Grand Patron gives them many presents."

He took a long breath and let it out.

"I don't want you to go back to them."

She kissed him gently, then moved away, shaking her head in a comedy of disbelief. Her hands moved over his body, caressing.

"Is it possible? Can I really believe you, monsieur? You want me only for yourself?" She gently tugged at his pyjama trousers, then with a firm tug pulled them off. "I would give anything to be admitted to the United States and to be your friend in Washington and visit all the famous monuments. In Washington, which is your favorite monument?"

SHE WAS SERPENT AND SIREN both.

He closed his eyes in anticipation of a first caress but when he opened them moments later the room's soft light was gone and so was she. Only the sliver of moon, and a finger of light at the bathroom door. She was in there, and to judge from the metallic yet furtive sounds was making a selection from among the many perfumes and ointments and sprays in the bathroom, as though she were a departing hotel guest.

"Do you know what I am doing, monsieur?"

"I think you're robbing the Grand Patron of a few souvenirs. But why just now?"

"I am preparing a feast for your body. Do you know the life of the dancer Mata Hari? She would anoint the body of her lovers with precious perfumes and oils. Or perhaps it was the dancer Salomé. You know about Madame Pompadour?

"Come back and be yourself. Mata Hari was shot and Salomé's friend lost his head."

She made several more trips to the bathroom, each time returning with perfume bottles, tubes and sprays in silver containers which she ranged in neat rows on the bedside table. She had put on a man's bathrobe of white silk, tied with a crimson sash. His body stirred in anticipation.

"Mata Hari was secretly loyal to the French. It was a mistake to shoot her." She took off the sash and put it over his eyes and insisted on tying it behind his head, tightly. "Mata Hari too was a victim. She was misunderstood."

"Like you?"

"Exactly."

She gave him a pat on the forehead, and a quick token squeeze that brought him sharply erect.

"Voilà! Now you are Ti Roro! Me too, I also am Ti Roro. I will be serpent and siren both."

She padded off, and he heard her rummaging in the closet where clothes were hanging. Clothes for both men and women guests.

"Which do you think the Grand Patron prefers. The boy or the girl?"

"Which do you, Gabrielle?"

She returned, and guided his hand. She was wearing tight men's trousers of a rough sailcoth.

"Feel my slim hips, monsieur. Could they not be the hips of Ti Roro? No, do not remove the sash!" She took his hand and laid it on one breast, then on the other. "Now I am siren and serpent both."

"I want to see. Whoever heard of a serpent with hips?"

"Be quiet, monsieur. It is I who will talk."

She lay beside him, still wearing the trousers and began to twist and turn. A rough sailcloth leg suddenly thrust over his hip momentarily crushed him.

"I ask you to pardon me. It was not intentional. I was reaching for the spray."

Leaning on an elbow that rested against his side, she tried out the spray, scattering a rich jasmine perfume. A cool yet astringent spray tickled his nipples, his navel, his penis. Gently with her left hand she pushed his penis aside to spray the balls. The spray burned.

"That is what Marie Antoinette said to her executioner when she stepped on his toe."

"What now?" he said impatiently.

"She said, 'I ask you to pardon me, monsieur. It was not intentional.' Isn't that splendid? The last words of her life! In some ways she was foolish but in other ways admirable."

He tugged at the sash binding his eyes. At last it came off. He kissed her. He was overwhelmed by the several perfumes.

"I don't want any French history. Not now, anyway. Where do you pick up all this stuff?"

"In school. The French schools are the best."

She lay beside him for a few moments then began to turn, slowly yet firmly until she was on top of him, but not lying there quietly, writhing instead as she imagined a serpent would writhe. She managed to be several places on top of him at once.

"Now I am Petit Roro the serpent. Think of yourself as the siren La Séductrice, about to surrender her body. The excited young boy approaches."

He slid out from under her and pushed her down, firmly.

"Now you want me to be La Séductrice? Very well, monsieur. I will be that young girl, almost a virgin."

"Let's don't exaggerate," he said. "Just be yourself."

She reached for one of the tubes and anointed him, first the nipples and the navel, then under the knees. An oily film, cool at first, began to sting, causing his skin to draw tight.

"This soft place is also a zone of pleasure, monsieur. Not everyone knows that." She kissed him gently, all the while rubbing him under his knees, first the right knee, then the left, then the right knee again. "How many young women are there in your office in Washington?"

"That's a secret," he said. "A military secret."

"I would like to be one of your secretaries and take down your words of dictation. No one would need to know about our secret relationship."

"What secret relationship?"

"After you have forgiven me we will have a secret relationship. At first in Paris but later in Washington. That is what I hope for."

She lay at last beneath him, no longer squirming.

THIS WAS NOT, HOWEVER, THE end of his long day.

monday

The Cultural Attaché

THE NEW RESPECT, ALMOST AWE, which the cultural attaché Gordon Seymour enjoyed following his successes of the preceding Monday had somewhat diminished during a frustrating week. The CIA station chief Trent and the Embassy security officer Chalmers spoke goodnaturedly of finding him a new office and secretary, but their hallway greetings took on a tone of friendly teasing. *"Look into any more Turkish toilets?"* *"Any new Sex Shops today?"* *"Still haven't found the femme de chambre?"* *"What gives with your French beanpole?"* Gordon continued to attend the daily meetings of the Embassy task force, but had no opinions to offer on the crank phone calls and patently absurd ransom demands flowing in from various Committees and Brigades and Movements,

174

most of them quite unknown. Only the misspelled assertions from two Basque separatist committees, probably the same group to judge from the rhetoric, seemed to him worthy of attention. But to the others in the task force this was the threat of a flea to an elephant. Basques kidnap an American Assistant Secretary of State! Impossible.

Gordon returned to the normal busy work of "cultural relations," which involved more vernissages and receptions than he cared to attend, and more visiting American dignitaries than he wanted to lunch with. But the late nights were his own. All his life he had taken long night walks when pondering enigmas of French history or when groping for new ideas for his lectures. So now in the warm summer nights he left his apartment on the rue Jacob for a round of favorite places. Through the Place Furstenberg to the rue de L'Abbaye, a glance at the tourists at the sidewalk tables of the Deux Magots, up the rue de Tournon to the delicately lit Odéon, then over to the Boulevard St. Michel and a beer or two at one of the sidewalk cafés and at last to the Seine quays, the brightly lit bateaux mouches gliding past Notre Dame, the lovers and the clochards, the barges. Near the Pont de Sully, on the fourth evening after the kidnapping, his attention was again caught by the barge *Don Carlos* of Santander. No one would ever know whether the young Joseph Conrad was shipwrecked after smuggling arms to the Carlist forces in northern Spain. Did he really have an affair with a mistress of the Pretender Don Carlos? Writers are professional liars, after all. Santander? Would some historian one day try to tell the life story of the turncoat Cuban terrorist Santander? An altogether emblematic story for the age of anarchy, to change sides five or six times with the changes of the Caribbean winds! A story he, Gordon, might some day find it amusing to write.

The *Princessa* of Bilbao was still moored to the quay. But the third barge that had caught his attention, the *Viscaya* of San Sebastián, was gone. Odd that a member of the *Viscaya* crew had cocked his rifle in response to his innocent questions. Sounded like a very old rifle indeed, perhaps a relic of the Spanish war. He walked on. Also odd, nagging at the fringes of consciousness since Monday, was the extraordinary behavior of the dentist Carlos Monzon and the journalist Georges Langlade at the Lutétia reception. The dentist's staring response, the dropped glass, their hasty exit immediately after hearing Pierre Perdoux refer to a Meurice femme de chambre and to François Bouquillon . . . all very strange. The death of Bouquillon remained an incomprehensible event, as elusive as ever after Pierre Perdoux's inquiries at the various French services. The French police and the DGSE dismissed any connection between a diplomat's kidnapping and the death of an obscure French sportswriter and gambler.

The cultural attaché walked on in the summer night, thinking, all the way to the Quai d'Ivry, then back by the Right Bank quays.

THE NEXT MORNING HE ASKED Perdoux to find everything in the French and Interpol files on the dentist Carlos Monzon and on the Cuban terrorist Santander. He went to the CIA station chief Trent with the same request. What did headquarters have on the two? And the FBI?

"Dr. Monzon? He's probably the favorite Paris dentist for Americans. And not just Paris Americans."

"I know, Trent. He did a root canal for me. He had me in earphones listening to music while he did it. Whenever the pain got bad I turned the volume up."

"So why Monzon? What are you thinking?"

"Just another hunch. The rich Cuban exiles have their fingers in a lot of pies. They are also unforgiving. At the Lutétia reception—"

"What about the Lutétia reception?"

"I was right once. Please do it. And while you're at it would you ask them for anything they have on Rolando Santander?"

"Santander? He's dead."

"Do me a favor and ask anyway."

TRENT WAS BACK AS THE Embassy offices were closing for the day, while it was still noon at CIA headquarters in Virginia. A sullen hot afternoon, the streets thronged with tourists in outlandish summer garb. First the staff officers, then the American secretaries, at last even the French underlings drifted off on one pretext or another. The building was a mausoleum.

"It was too late to have anyone go through the FBI raw file."

"How about Langley?"

"More or less what you'd expect of a patriot. Monzon left Cuba in fifty-nine, six months after Castro came to power. His father was one of the biggest sugar people, a showcase mill near Havana and half a dozen others over the island. He left school, Rollins College in Florida, to train for the Bay of Pigs operation. He was one of those who didn't get captured. After dental school he set up quite a practice in Miami. The rich Cuban exiles, but also big shots from abroad. He went to Managua to treat a couple of Somozas. Santo Domingo and Haiti, too. The traveling dentist, just like now."

"Politics?"

"He was a leader in the Cuban community in Miami.

Chairman of committees, the Chamber of Commerce, once a delegate to the OAS. Chaired a commission on human rights abuses."

"That's all? I think you're holding back something. Did he work for the Company somewhere along the line? Or for the DEA?"

"I'm telling you what they told me."

"And Santander?"

"They didn't say anything. Just that he disappeared two years ago."

Pierre Perdoux was back the next morning with a small cahier full of scribbled notes. He began to enumerate different intelligence services concerned with the struggle against terrorism.

"There are seven, each with its files. The Direction centrale de la police judiciare, the DCRG, the RGPP, the BRI—"

"Never mind," Gordon interrupted. "What about the JUDEX data?"

"Unfortunately there was a failure of electric current."

"So what are all these notes, Pierre?"

"These are from other investigations. However, I can tell you this, confidentially, of course. Santander entered France two years ago from Mexico on a tourist visa good for three months. There is no evidence that he has left France. His situation is therefore irregular and leaves him subject to arrest and deportation."

"And nothing on Carlos Monzon?"

"His situation is regular. He has permission to reside and to practice dentistry. I learned this much from a friend in my own service. He has treated several men high in the Ministry of Foreign Affairs. Not only rich Americans."

"And Interpol?"

"I spent two hours in waiting rooms. They insisted I lacked the necessary authorization. Unfortunately I could not reach my superiors to have them confirm I was legitimate. It was very humiliating, all that. I intend to return today."

So Pierre Perdoux was mired in the abyss of bureaucracy, and the CIA was stonewalling. At two o'clock, eight o'clock in the morning in New York, Gordon phoned a young assistant professor, one of his best graduate students and one of the last scholars to repeatedly cite his own work in French history, to check through the *New York Times* Index for entries on Carlos Monzon and Rolando Santander. And if possible go to the microfilmed newspaper itself. If not, the index summaries would do.

The young professor returned his call shortly after midnight, and not long after Gordon had returned from his round of St. Germain, the Odéon, St. Michel, the quays.

His investigation had been satisfactory, even intriguing. In 1967 Dr. Monzon was practicing in New Orleans, not Miami, and was arrested, tried and acquitted on the charge of beating a girlfriend to death in a Metairie apartment. Her mouth had been stuffed, probably after death, with her long blonde hair. The girlfriend's apartment was full of souvenirs from the young dentist's travels, but there was no corroborating evidence. Later Monzon was chairman of a committee investigating human rights abuses in Cuba, and had been an "observer" at meetings of the Organization of American States.

The terrorist activities of Rolando Santander were recorded over three decades, often in two- and three-inch stories. The names of Monzon and the terrorist twice appeared in the same *Times* stories. Both men were among half a dozen exiles charged by a leftist think tank with involvement in two plots to assassinate Castro, one of these the famous enterprise of the exploding cigar. On the other occasion they were charged but not tried for attempted assassination of a deviant leader of the Contras, Monzon as one of the planners, Santander as an active participant. This event had occurred during a Monzon vacation in Honduras. In the explosion which failed to liquidate the rebellious Contra leader Santander's own legs were crushed.

The young professor had spent a profitable day.

This was on Friday. Pierre Perdoux declined to work over the weekend, pleading family obligations. And Gordon failed to get an appointment with Dr. Monzon. On Monday morning, the same Monday morning that took the Assistant Secretary to the Grand Patron's villa in Cap Ferrat, Gordon met with Perdoux for a cup of coffee in the Embassy cafeteria, to be followed by a conference in his office. Gordon had brought with him copies of the *International Herald Tribune* and *Le Monde*, Pierre Perdoux had a copy of *Le Figaro*. Each was eager to glance through the headlines before beginning their discussion.

It was Perdoux who discovered the small boxed story of the highjacked barge *Viscaya*, an amusing fait divers, a moment's comic relief from the sombre litany of economic failure, overcrowded highways and starvation in the Sudan. An oddity, the *Figaro* noted, that would have delighted Flaubert. Perdoux burst out laughing, and pointed to the headline.

LE DUC DE CLARENCE AU CANAL
DE LOING. BAIN DE CALVADOS.

Three Basque sailors had been locked in the galley of a barge named *Viscaya*, moored for the night near the village of La Morinière, not far from Montargis. They had attempted to escape by opening an emergency door to one of the vats of apple brandy, could not close the door and had nearly drowned. They had spent the night immersed in brandy, repeatedly tasting the surrounding liquid in order to keep warm. The sailors claimed they had been tied up at gunpoint by an American criminal and a young French woman of easy virtue.

"I ask myself, who is the Duke of Clarence?"

"A thirsty Englishman who drowned in a butt of malmsey wine," Gordon said. "I think we have found the Assistant Secretary."

It was not yet nine in the Embassy cafeteria. By eleven they were at the CAFÉ TABAC in La Morinière, where Gordon immediately recognized the anomalous framed portraits of the Duvaliers father and son. Papa Doc and Baby Doc in an isolated French hamlet! Could the Assistant Secretary, if it was indeed he, now be a prisoner of Haitian sadists? Worse things might happen. But not many. The French woman of easy virtue was undoubtedly the Meurice femme de chambre Gabrielle Soubiran. But why, if she was party to the kidnapping, had she helped the Assistant Secretary escape from the barge? The proprietor of the café was willing enough to talk about the American "criminal" and his little tramp.

"They were right here, in my café, sitting where you are sitting. The man wanted to telephone Paris but didn't have a franc. Ordered drinks and didn't have a sou to pay for them."

"Telephone Paris?"

"He was out of his head. He said he was the kidnapped American diplomat. He phoned collect to the American officials in Paris but they wouldn't take his call. Even the Americans can't pay for every degenerate who appeals to them for money. He was no more a diplomat than I am."

"Where did they go?"

"He was taken to the chateau."

Minutes later they were in the decaying chateau. Here Perdoux's police credentials and several sharp slaps broke through the reserve of Dieudonné Joseph, the tall white-robed "medical man" who met them in the salon of ruined furniture and roosting chickens. Gordon described Randall as an eccentric friend who had a tendency to wander off.

"Of course I have seen your friend. He was our guest. I may have saved his life, at the very least his arm. He had a terrible infection. It was necessary to operate."

"Operate?"

"Only the thumb. It is possible he will lose more."

"Describe him," Perdoux commanded.

"Don't speak to me in that manner. I am a medical man."

The description corresponded well enough. The curling hair and workman's clothes could have been ways of disguising a prisoner.

"Where is he now?"

"The maître took him away in his car. Your friend wanted to see a French doctor. What could a French doctor do more than I? It's possible the maître took him to the clinic in Montbard."

"I think he is here in the chateau," Perdoux said. "Take us through."

They were shown every room, even the medical man's "reception room," where two scared women squatted on the stone floor, even the voodoo shrine with a black madonna whose thin golden arms reached above her head to become a halo. At last they were taken to the attic atelier of the frail painter Philomé Hauteville, who was at work on Degas dancers. Frail and diabetic, but he had the courage to defy Dieudonné Joseph.

"He was here for one night, the next night he was downstairs with his woman. Then the maître took them away. The maître was taking them south."

"You are a cretin who knows nothing of what goes on in the world," Joseph said. "How can you know anything locked up in your tower?"

"Everyone knows the maître was taking them south. Ask any of the servants."

Gordon looked at the paintings. Copies of famous French paintings and one wall of superb primitives in the blues and bright yellows of Haitian painting.

"You are a splendid painter, monsieur." He nodded to the primitives.

"Those daubs are nothing. My true work is this, these beautiful young dancers of the Paris opera. They were painted by Degas. I have also copied Courbet, Monet and Cézanne. I copy all the great painters."

Gordon inspected the Degas.

"I congratulate you on your choice of painters. What is your name?"

"Philomé Hauteville."

"Of course you are right, Monsieur Hauteville, everyone knows the maître took them south, that goes without saying. It was to Jean-Claude Duvalier near Cannes, was it not?"

"Of course not," Dieudonné Joseph interrupted. "The old revolutionary doesn't know anything. The maître was taking them to the Grand Patron at St. Jean Cap Ferrat."

The painter shrugged his thin shoulders.

"You are not the first to look for that American. The maître's dentist also came from Paris to look for him. Why is everyone looking for this man if he is only a degenerate?"

"You will be flogged," Joseph said. "What do you know about what goes on in the world?"

"I know what I know. And I am free to look out the

window. Those men came in a black car as long as the maître's."

"What's the dentist's name?" Gordon asked Dieudonné Joseph.

"How should I know?"

Perdoux slapped him again.

"His name is Dr. Carlos Monzon. He comes to the chateau from Paris twice a year to examine the maître's teeth and to add more gold."

"Did you tell Dr. Monzon what you have told us?"

"Why not? Dr. Monzon is a friend of the house. He will follow them to the Grand Patron."

"One more question. What is the Grand Patron's name?"

"Toussaint Bazile," Joseph said. "Everyone knows that."

THEY WERE IN NICE BY nine o'clock after the fast five hundred miles from Auxerre, where they had a quick snack and Gordon telephoned the CIA station chief. A discreet conversation, since the phone was within earshot of the cashier. He told Trent he had acquired the information he needed. He would, however, appreciate the help of one or two good "accountants" and hoped they would meet him in Nice, at the Negresco, tonight in fact. Perdoux, who had only a croque monsieur and a glass of a recent Nuits at Auxerre, watched in dismay as they sped within minutes of the Auberge Bressane of Mâcon, the Ermitage on the outskirts of Lyon, the Bec Fin at Vienne. Modest establishments all, but all meriting an hour's pause. Even an early dinner at La Licorne in Valence, not the world famous Pic, would have improved morale. But Gordon drove implacably on. It was not yet nine when they approached the white splendor of the Negresco, and the line of chauffeurs smoking beside the Ferraris, the Mercedes, the Rolls. One of the Rolls was a startling white convertible. Not unlike the one brought from Colombia by the drug lord Roque Amador, and featured in the last issue of *Paris-Match*.

At the concierge's station, and in the act of unfolding a map, was Dr. Monzon and beside him Georges Langlade. The journalist touched the dentist's sleeve, the dentist looked up from his map. He took off his dark glasses to verify this appalling apparition: the cultural attaché and the foolish looking scarecrow French agent of the Lutétia reception. Gordon offered to shake hands, but the dentist recoiled.

"What in the devil are you doing in Nice?"

"Just a three-day holiday," Gordon said. "You too? Or are you seeing a patient?"

"What did you say? A patient?"

"Hypollite Jasmin, for instance?"

The dentist put the dark glasses back on.

"I don't know what you're talking about, Mr. Seymour."

"You don't have a patient by that name?"

"Not in Nice."

"Of course not. He is your patient at La Morinière, I think. But sometimes patients move about. A good dentist follows them."

The dentist stared.

"What are you? La Morinière? What do you know about La Morinière? How dare you ask questions about my patients? What business is it of yours what I do and where I go?" Monzon turned to Perdoux, who appeared to be examining with curiosity the lavish vestibule and beyond it the streaming lights of the Promenade des Anglais.

"Just vulgar curiosity," Gordon said.

The dentist looked past him as at a pursuing fiend.

"We'll go to my room, Georges," he said. "This cultural attaché has no manners."

ONCE BEFORE GORDON HAD COME to Nice on a mission to track down a vanished dignitary. He was twenty-two then, his hair was brown not gray, and his quarry was one Robert Barnave, an anti-Semitic writer and executive secretary of a Vichy cabinet minister. That was in the heady days when OSS, CID and army intelligence could still operate independently of French authorities. At the time it was not clear to Gordon why his superiors wanted to protect this man from the French, who would certainly have brought him to trial. His job was simply to find Barnave. It would be someone else's job to take him in hand. Years later, thirty years later in fact, it came out that Barnave had been a useful conduit of information on communist leaders in the Franc Tireurs et Partisans resistance group. That was why the OSS felt obligated to protect him. The guilt of his complicity nagged at Gordon from time to time over the years, although Barnave was no Klaus Barbie. At twenty-two Gordon had enjoyed the excitement of the chase, and the game of concealment. His cover was to be one of a team making an economic survey of conditions in the south of France.

On that December evening, thanks to a trail of sleazy informants, from Paris and Clermont-Ferrand to Marseille, Gordon found the fugitive in the labyrinth of Vieux Nice. He was huddled in a miserable unheated third-floor room of a fifth-rate walkup hotel. The anti-Semite, who was not privy to Gordon's intentions, thought he was about to be arrested if not killed. In his terror he began to vomit and babbled excuses while the vomit trickled over his chin.

He went back to the old city tonight, leaving Perdoux in the hotel and his car parked at the port. He went out of curiosity, drawn by an almost forgotten taste for risk and the clandestine, the amusing disreputable game of secrecy and disguise. Strange feelings, first awakened by the quite unexpected invitation to join the crisis task-force meeting at the Embassy. Only seven days ago! Tomorrow agents would be down from Paris to take over, were perhaps already in Nice. But tonight he was on his own. So he went back to the cobblestoned streets and dank alleys of the old city, and even unerringly to the walkup hotel, only two rooms wide, where he had found Barnave. It was not a hotel now, no HOTEL PALACE nameplate, no promise of *Tout Confort*. Only a doorway almost blocked by a garbage can and a glazed ground-floor window announcing rooms to rent. A dark hallway and corkscrew stairs.

A florid woman in hair curlers stopped him. She was in worn slippers and rolled silk stockings that almost reached her knees. Her kimono was open over faded pink underwear and safety pins.

"What are you looking for?" she asked, using the familiar *tu*. She examined his gray hairs. "There's nothing of all that here."

"I was here long ago, madame. I'd like to see a third-floor room where I was as a young man. A bit of nostalgia."

"What are you after, monsieur? For the drug or the girl you must go elsewhere." She came closer, as though to smell his breath. "I think you are the police, no? You're not French, are you?"

"American."

"You are looking for the little American writer? He hasn't done anything. Just fills his pieces of paper and then throws them away and lives off the earnings of his slut Simone. A writer, that? He's on the fifth floor not the third.''

He gave her a fifty-franc bill.

"It's a room on the third I want to see."

Her massive shoulders stirred, a hunch of one shoulder, then the other.

"If the *locataire* is awake, yes. Sometimes he never gets up." She rubbed the bill appraisingly. Would it be possible to extract another? "On the other hand, if you only want to see the room, why not? You Americans are sentimental."

He followed her up the corkscrew stairway, circling into fetid darkness. At the third-floor landing there were two doors side by side. She knocked at the door at the left, two quick knocks, then struggled to fit the key.

"It's occupied, madame!" a squeaky voice responded.

"It's the other door," Gordon said. "The one on the right."

"Nothing of interest there, just a storeroom," she said, turning the key. An emaciated old man in an orange sweat-shirt was sitting on the edge of the bed. Long gray underwear reached his feet, which were groping for slippers. A few wisps of beard hung over the neck of the sweatshirt, which had a printed picture of Beethoven.

"Leave me alone," the old man said. "I've paid for the whole month, I have the right to be left alone."

"It's a mistake," Gordon said, thinking of the terrified Barnave. "It's the other room I wanted to see."

She shrugged and tucked his fifty-franc bill under her faded brassiere.

"What is it with you, monsieur? There's nothing to see in that room."

They went back out onto the landing and she tried several keys.

"There's no way," she said at last.

"Perhaps you have other keys downstairs."

She shook her head, too busy for further nonsense.

"It's only a storeroom. I assure you there's nothing to see."

He went back to his car, not his car after all, a car with Embassy plates. And the taste for risk was still there in his mouth, in his mind, and the intoxicating illusion of reliving a deep past. At twenty-two he would have gone on, alone, to find the Grand Patron's place and even reconnoitre a little. He got in the car, amused at his vagrant impulse, and headed toward the Promenade des Anglais and his room in the Negresco, then changed his mind and turned back in the direction of Villefranche and Cap Ferrat. Only six miles, not even that, he would be back at the hotel by midnight.

A CAFÉ WAS OPEN AT the land end of Cap Ferrat, a few hundred feet from the bus stop. A lone waiter was stacking chairs. He asked for the villa of the Haitian Toussaint Bazile.

"Of course I know it. Who doesn't? It's like an army camp up there. Blacks with machine guns and a big fence."

"Hard to find?"

"It's complicated. You don't see much until you're right on top of it, even though it's very big. Unless they have the floodlights on."

Gordon extracted another fifty-franc bill.

"Why don't you come with me and show the way? Then I'll bring you back."

"No thanks. I mind my own business."

The narrow side road, marked with arrows for two estates, one Villa Bon Aventure, the other Villa Monséjour, climbed steeply away from the corniche road. A hundred yards into the sideroad a black man in uniform stepped into the car's lights. He had a submachine gun.

"It's this way for Monsieur Bazile?"

"You are invited?"

"Of course."

The guard grinned and made a steep bow.

"Straight ahead, the second on your left. No problem, you will see the gate."

He drove past the second lane, not slowing, and parked the car in a thick grove. To the left, through the trees, he could make out a high metal fence guarding Villa Bon Aventure. On the other side the overgrown land climbed steadily to Villa Monséjour, a large dark mansion with several turrets, One of these was lit. The shadow of a man crossed and recrossed the single turret window, like a guard.

He walked back toward the lane leading to the gate to Villa Bon Aventure. At the gate two blacks stepped out of a sentry box. One had a large revolver in his belt, the other a submachine gun. From somewhere beyond the sentry box two arrows of light probed for a few moments before centering on himself. He was half-blinded but could still make out a long white villa with lights on two floors.

The guards said nothing.

"I was out for a walk," Gordon said. "This is the villa of Monsieur Bazile?"

"Why do you ask?"

"Monsieur Bazile is a great and famous man. It is interesting to see the villas of the rich. It must be a privilege for you to work for him!"

The two guards looked at each other and grinned. A rapid exchange in Creole. He did not understood a word.

"I am an admirer of the Haitian people," Gordon said. "It must be sad to be so far away from your beautiful homeland."

"It's not so bad. At least we eat."

Gordon took out his billfold. He held a hundred-franc bill

up to the light. Even the numbers showed in the glaring light.

"Monsieur Bazile is a great man and must have many visitors. I believe Monsieur Hypollite Jasmin is a visitor. Do you have other visitors now?"

The guards looked at the hundred-franc bill still bathed in light.

"What is that to you?"

It was the guard with the submachine gun. The other stepped forward, and reached for the bill, a swift animal claw. He stuffed it in a hip pocket, grinning. The first guard growled. They were all caught in the bright arrows of light.

"Now it's mine! It's to me he is speaking. It's me he paid."

"Divide," the other guard said. "You have to divide."

"What time is it?" the first guard asked, looking at Gordon's wristwatch.

"Eleven-fifteen."

"Let's see the watch!"

It was a barked command. Gordon held the watch up to the light.

"I said let me see it. Take it off!"

Gordon turned to leave. Should he walk or make a run for it? If he gave up the watch they would next demand his wallet, his credit cards, his identity, everything.

"You must pardon me for bothering you," he said. "I'll come back in the morning to call on Monsieur Bazile. He is a good friend of one of my good friends, an important banker in Paris. Monsieur Bazile will be delighted to see me."

The two guards conferred. A barrage of Creole, both talking at once. Then a long silence. Apparently they had decided to forego his watch but not return the hundred francs.

"Are you telling the truth? Tomorrow we will see if you are telling the truth. Telephone before you come back. We will see what Monsieur Bazile has to say. Tonight he is not here."

Two hundred yards, more or less, to the car. He began to trot toward it and was quickly out of breath. Not the lungs or heartbeats of twenty-two.

A single rifle shot rang out, as if to punctuate a warning, just as he reached the car, then several shots skittering in the underbrush only a few feet away.

HE GOT IN THE CAR and drove back to Nice, fast. He was still several blocks away, on the Promenade des Anglais, when he saw the flashing lights of police cars and a small crowd gathered on the sidewalk at the entrance to the Negresco. An ambulance had nosed into the back of the crowd. Wailing sirens were approaching.

On the sidewalk, framed in floodlight, a long Mercedes limousine hunched forward like an animal brought violently to its knees. The front of the car was in shreds but the rest of the body, though covered by shining metallic fragments, was virtually intact. From a hole torn in the roof, or perhaps simply from the sunroof opened to the warm night, a man's head protruded. It was all there to the top of the neck, the eyes open and even calm and contemplative, the head resting flat as though neatly decapitated and then placed on the roof for the convenience of photographers. The photographers were already at work.

Gordon knew that face, a dentist's face, even before the man who had seized his elbow began to repeat the two names in a frenetic chant.

"Mr. Seymour, Mr. Seymour! Dr. Monzon, Dr. Monzon!"

In death, and in the light from the police cars, the face of

Dr. Monzon was no longer mischievous, and there was no sign of the dark glasses.

The man clutching his elbow was Georges Langlade.

"I want protection," he whispered. "Take me to your room, Mr. Seymour. You Embassy people are safe, no one would dare touch you, even Roque Amador would not touch you, the French will not touch you. You are neutral, you are always outside things. No violence, right? Listen to me, Mr. Seymour, I too am neutral. Only a journalist, only an observer who tried to help the Assistant Secretary. I want immunity and protection. I will tell you everything, Mr. Seymour. Everything! But only if I am protected."

Gordon hesitated only moments. It would not take long, not more than ten or fifteen minutes, for the police to discover that the journalist Langlade had arrived in Nice only hours before in the company of the late Dr. Monzon. After that, who knew when he would get to see him?

Where was Pierre Perdoux now that he really needed him? And where was Trent? He should have arrived in Nice by now. Paris was only an hour's flight.

"Room 312," he said. "Wait ten minutes before coming."

"Ten minutes! It wouldn't take Amador five to kill me."

"Amador blew up the car? Roque Amador?"

"Of course. You see the white Rolls by the ambulance? Even a Colombian license plate. *Carro de la muerte!* That's his signature, he never even hides his presence at the scene. Listen to me, Mr. Seymour. It will be the Grand Patron's turn next if not mine. Or yours! Amador will stop at nothing to get his hands on the Assistant Secretary."

tuesday

The Roman Ruins

THE ASSISTANT SECRETARY AND GABRIELLE were, shortly after midnight, reclining on a thick white rug in the Salle des Jeux, watching acrobats on a variety program from Monte Carlo. They were at ease in Chinese silk robes from the inexhaustible closet of their guest room. The television set had been placed in the cut-out center of an eighteenth-century erotic painting so as to give a trompe l'oeil illusion that the two lovers of the painting, who were reclined on a Louis XVI lit de repos, the man wearing only a red jacket, the woman only stockings, were also watching television. Beside the Assistant Secretary and Gabrielle on the rug, Ti Roro and La Séductrice were playing a game they called "Brother and Sister." They writhed in time with the music,

194

one then the other on top, brown legs entangled with coiling arms that multiplied with the dexterity of bronzed Eastern idols. Their naked brown bodies were never still.

"They are young," Gabrielle said, while gently stroking the Assistant Secretary's good hand, "Their eccentricities must be excused. They were brought up in the tropics. You know the picture book *Paul et Virginie*?"

"No."

"The young boy and girl live in the tropics and have natural goodness until they come to France and must submit to conventions. They were brother and sister who had no fear of incest. I think that was the story."

Her foot nudged the slim buttocks of La Séductrice, which at the moment were the closest.

"Are you two brother and sister?"

"Don't know," Ti Roro muttered. "How about you and your American?"

Gabrielle laughed. She gave the Assistant Secretary a quick squeeze.

"He is more like my father, no? In Washington we will have a secret relationship and we will tell the Americans he is my father. Then they will have no nasty suspicions."

La Séductrice looked up from her exertions.

"Is that true, monsieur? You will take Gabrielle to the United States?"

For the moment it even seemed like a good idea. He had stopped resisting her delicate and ingenious caresses. Why bother to argue with her fantasies?

"How can I take her anywhere if the Grand Patron keeps us prisoner?"

"That is a precaution," Ti Roro said. "The Grand Patron wants us all to go to New York. You and Gabrielle, all of us. We will all go on a luxury Concorde from Paris to New York.

In front of the plane will be Jean-Claude Duvalier and his wife. The rest of us behind."

"And after that?"

"Hollywood, Disneyland, Florida, Las Vegas. All this will happen as soon as we have permission to enter the United States. The Grand Patron has promised we will not be left behind."

"You will arrange it," Gabrielle said, giving the Assistant Secretary a hug. "No problem. In Washington I will work in your office without pay, only enough for my little necessities. Whenever you wish to communicate with the French government you will dictate to me your thoughts and I will make the necessary corrections in the grammar."

The Assistant Secretary returned her hug. His good hand slipped under the Kimono for a friendly stroking. An image floated on the screen, next to the two acrobats in gaudy spacesuits, of Gabrielle jogging on the Mall, entering a Georgetown restaurant, opening the door to her apartment, greeting him. It was hard to believe none of that would ever happen.

He did not relish the thought of her going to prison.

"How much will they cost, the little necessities?"

"Almost nothing."

The acrobats on the screen suddenly disappeared. The program was interrupted by a newscast. Terrorism in Nice, a Cuban dentist blown up in his Mercedes, right in front of the Negresco. The camera found its way past spectators and police to a macabre close-up: a man's head apparently severed from the body and resting on top of a wrecked car. The man's eyes were open. The car had evidently been exploded by remote control. Dr. Carlos Monzon of Paris, 52, born in Havana, Cuba, dentist, 12 Avenue Montaigne. Two bystanders were slightly injured. Beyond the ambulances and police cars were the Ferraris, the Daimlers, a white Rolls-Royce convertible.

"My God," Gabrielle said. "That is the terrorist the Grand Patron was protecting us from!" She addressed the two orphans, who had ceased their play and were staring at the screen. "Did he do it, the Grand Patron? He is not here this evening."

Ti Roro shrugged his thin shoulders.

"Anything is possible. He knows his way around, the Grand Patron."

"What do you think, monsieur? You have experience with the great world."

Randall's mind reverted to the cells only a few feet beneath them, and the naked Hypollite Jasmin. And to burning cars in Salvador, Guatemala, Honduras. The Chilean attaché in Washington. It was relatively easy to blow up a car.

"The Grand Patron likes to have his way."

"But he is a man of culture," Gabrielle protested. "How could he blow up a dentist?"

"And the car," Ti Roro said. "Don't forget the car."

MEANWHILE THE GRAND PATRON, RETURNING from dinner in Cap d'Antibes, had also seen the head of the late Dr. Monzon resting on the roof of a Mercedes in many ways similar to his own. He too had been watching the acrobats on the small screen encased in the partition separating him from his bodyguard and driver. His hands, which had been keeping time with the hands of the acrobats, turned clammy and cold. The car had just passed the Nice airport and in only minutes would reach the Negresco. On the one hand he felt a normal desire to see the inert head of the arrogant Cuban on the top of a car. It would certainly remain there for many minutes more as the police took their photographs and made their diagrams. On the other hand, it was hardly a good place for him to be seen. No one was above suspicion. It would be far more prudent to turn inland to the Autoroute, which passed high above Nice. Or to stop at the seaside airport and make himself noisily, even obnoxiously, visible at the Ciel d'Azur restaurant.

On the small screen the camera moved over the faces of the crowd, the police cars and ambulances, the white stone and blue awnings of the Negresco and its balcony, and up the narrow street where the cars of the millionaires waited.

Among them was the white Rolls convertible of Roque Amador. The Grand Patron knew whose Rolls that was. It had merited a half-page in *Paris-Match*. How many white Rolls convertibles cross the Atlantic in the belly of a private plane?

His longing for the security of Villa Bon Aventure became intense. His locked gates, his faithful guards, his little companions Ti Roro and La Séductrice, who looked up to him as to a father. A man's good deeds should be added in the balance, also his personal sacrifices on behalf of the President-for-Life. The Grand Patron had always loved order, he had always respected authority. One did what one could.

He turned off the television. He wanted no further glimpses of the Amador Rolls-Royce. It was evident he must rid himself of the stupid Randall at once, together with his scatter-brained poule, and Hypollite Jasmin for that matter. Get them off his place! Not even the vacant cells in the cellar would be safe. The gates of Bon Aventure must be open to welcome the Colombian beast, who would be invited to inspect every room. And even so... would it not instead be prudent to forestall that visit and turn the American over to Amador at once? Tonight, in fact? Why not ask Amador for a round million, francs not dollars, but be willing to accept less? A token payment, as it were, to salvage honor. Yet even the thought of coming face to face with the Colombian *trafficeur* was disagreeable. Perhaps all could be arranged by telephone.

The Grand Patron, feeling very cold in the Mercedes now gliding high above the lights of Nice, turned off the air conditioning. He wanted to be home in bed.

HE MADE THE CALL FROM the privacy of his bedroom dominated by an eighteenth century four-poster bed normally shared with Ti Roro and La Séductrice. They were not there tonight, in fact they were nowhere to be seen. The Assistant Secretary and the Innocent had also retired, which was just as well. The Grand Patron stared at his white bedside telephone, then at the antique telephone on his desk. All around him were the comforts acquired by a patriotic concern for order and by undeviating loyalty to the father François and the son Jean-Claude. The cherubs on the painted ceiling looked down on him, an heroic bust by Houdon admonished him to be brave, his sofa of Genoese velvet counseled delay, his unique copy of the Louvre hermaphrodite spoke of menaced delights.

He telephoned.

A long twenty minutes later his call was returned, Amador himself speaking. In the background were the sounds of raucous drunken celebration. Two Spanish voices in friendly argument against the sound of music turned up very loud.

"I am listening," Amador said.

"You know who I am, señor?"

"Of course. I intended to pay you a visit very soon. Possibly tomorrow."

"I think I know what you want." The Grand Patron was astounded by his own audacity. "There's no need to come here. We can make other arrangements."

A flood of Spanish silenced the room. He assumed Amador was now alone.

"They say you have a splendid villa on Cap Ferrat. I would like to see it."

"I would be delighted to show it to you. Any time. But I would first like to rid myself of my guest."

"Monzon told me about your guest." A long silence, then the sounds of Amador pouring himself a drink, crushing an ice cube with his teeth. "You heard what happened tonight?"

"Yes."

"The line between life and death is thin. It makes a man reflect."

"Exactly. My feeling, señor, is that my guest would be more useful in your hands than in mine. Your grievances are more serious. In fact I propose turning him over to you tonight, also the little French woman if you want her. You know about the femme de chambre?"

Amador laughed. The sounds ensued of his taking a long drink, then more sounds of teeth cracking ice. Would it be like that, the sounds of bones cracking on a medieval rack? The *trafficeurs* probably had racks.

"Tonight? Why not tomorrow?"

"I trust my intuitions, señor. It should be tonight. My guest belongs with you."

"You are an intelligent man, Bazile."

"Thank you, excellency. I would, however, like a little something in return for the risks I have taken. Say a million."

"Dollars?"

What was the meaning of that long drawn-out word, pronounced in rolling Spanish not French? Amusement or anger? A million dollars was nothing to a man of Amador's fortune.

"Say five hundred thousand. Dollars, of course."

"I never travel with cash."

"No problem, señor. Your word is enough."

A discussion of details. The Grand Patron proposed the last curve of the D914 before the isolated village of St. Pancrace, five miles inland from Nice. At that hour the famous Rotisserie would be closed and every house in the village dark. Amador objected. Even the smallest secondary road could mean unexpected interference. Witnesses. The Grand Patron then proposed the Roman ruins in Cimiez. Not more than ten minutes from the Negresco, but certain to be as solitary at that hour as an abandoned farm a half-hour inland.

It was arranged. The two cars would proceed to the rendezvous at three-thirty, less than three hours away, the Grand Patron's envoy in a Mercedes, Amador's in a Thunderbird. At that time Amador's man would give a promissory note for five hundred thousand dollars. The actual transfer of persons to take place at exactly three-thirty between the entrance to the Roman ruins and the Museum of the Villa des Arènes. The rendezous to be fifty meters beyond the museum.

"Only one man and one car," Amador said.

"Of course. I will send a trusted lieutenant, Hypollite Jasmin. And on your side, señor?"

"Also one man and one car." He crushed more ice. "Probably myself."

The humiliated Hypollite Jasmin, still naked under a coarse blanket, was astonished to be awakened at two o'clock in the morning by the Grand Patron himself, unlocking his cell. All was forgiven. He had, in fact, been chosen to deliver the American and the French *poule* to a representative of the President-for-Life. The transfer was to occur in an isolated place, the Roman ruins of Cimiez, so as to avoid any risk of interference. This very night, three-thirty in the morning.

"You are being honored, Jasmin. But what my hand gives it can also take away."

"I will never forget this moment, Grand Patron. But why Cimiez? Why not drive them all the way to the President-for-Life?"

"Too far. Too many chances to be stopped. There have been several roadblocks this week."

"What car am I taking to Cimiez?"

"Your own Mercedes. That will make you eager to respect my instructions and scrupulously avoid the police."

THE ASSISTANT SECRETARY WAS AWAKENED twice. The first time was by Ti Roro, who had slid onto the bottom of the bed and was slowly pushing his way between the sleeping Gabrielle and himself. The boy tapped Randall's left knee several times, gently, as though to announce his presence. The long nail of his index finger moved slowly up his thigh in the direction of the loins, then downward to the knee, this followed by a soft brushing motion of the palm of the hand, also up and down. The Assistant Secretary briefly kept his eyes closed, as to prolong a pleasant dream, then opened them to see that the boy, who was naked, was now kneeling between them, and that he was administering the same caresses to Gabrielle, but to her stomach rather than thigh. The nail moving up and down, followed by the palm. Gabrielle's skin was blue in the soft light, so too the boy's shoulders. His penis was a long erect shadow. Her breathing had become irregular in response to the nail and hand. Her head turned toward the Assistant Secretary but her eyes remained closed. She sighed.

"Don't disturb yourself, monsieur," Ti Roro whispered. "There is room for us all. I will enter her while she sleeps."

The Assistant Secretary was momentarily tempted by this perversity, but quickly recovered as the image of his Washington office again intruded. Someone was going through the papers on his desk. He pushed the boy away.

The second time he was awakened by the Grand Patron himself. A gloved hand stroked his shoulder, the straw hat glistened in the moonlight.

"You must get up at once, monsieur. I am no longer able to protect you. The drug chieftain Roque Amador is a madman. Tonight he killed poor Monzon, tomorrow it could be you. We must get you to a safe place in stronger hands than mine."

"Whose hands?"

"The hands of the President-for-Life. With him you are as safe as if you were in La Citadelle. We will take you to him tonight. Hypollite Jasmin will take you."

"Jasmin!"

"He has been forgiven. A leader must rule with an iron hand. But he must also be ready to forgive. Unexpected forgiveness is as terrifying as punishment. One or the other would bind him to me for life."

The Assistant Secretary looked down on the sleeping Gabrielle. Was she lying beside him for the last time? He rubbed her shoulder gently until she awoke. She sat up, startled to see the Grand Patron hovering there, the straw hat, the gloves, the teeth. She covered her breasts with the sheet.

The Assistant Secretary thought about the several occasions when a tone of authority had silenced Latino foreign ministers, even colonels. The time had come to be firm. But he was naked, whereas the Grand Patron was fully dressed. The tone of authority eluded him.

"Why not just get it over with and release me? You have treated me decently, I'll even go along with the farce and say you've been 'protecting' me. But not after tonight. This is your chance to be in the clear. So why not have Jasmin drive me into Nice and drop me off?"

"Me too, monsieur! Don't forget Gabrielle."

The Grand Patron gave the covered breasts a speculative glance.

"You would be better off with me, mademoiselle. In Nice the authorities would arrest you."

"Not at all. I will tell them that I too was a victim. Monsieur Randall will confirm this. He is now my friend."

The Grand Patron dismissed this with a wave.

"Of course you will be released, monsieur, perhaps even tomorrow. But not by me. The moral authority of the President-for-Life will protect you. He is known in Washington. They will listen to his reasonable demands."

"They won't listen to either of you. Your chance right now is to save your skin. Take us into Nice and let us go."

The Grand Patron drew himself up. He looked very tall and austere. He began to take off his gloves.

"You are to get up at once. The car will leave in ten minutes."

"Let me talk to Washington. It's still early in the evening there. I'll try to work out a deal for you."

"I must ask you to get out of bed. Take the Innocent with you or leave her with me, the choice is yours."

"I'm going with him," Gabrielle said.

THE CAR GLIDED THROUGH THE villa gates and onto a small lane. The lounging guards stood up and saluted, then closed the gates behind them. Ahead they saw the scattered lights of Villefranche. The back doors were locked from in front, the dividing window was bulletproof and to be opened only by remote control, the side windows were opaque. They were in a warm and impenetrable prison of glass. Even at midday the Assistant Secretary and Gabrielle would be only shadows to anyone peering in.

"At least you are not now in the trunk, monsieur." She tugged at the armrest, and he helped her push it back. She gave his knee a squeeze. "This way it is more intimate."

"What are you looking for?"

"The telecommand. Without it we cannot look at T.V. or have drinks from the bar. Also it operates the windows and the partition."

She tapped at the glass dividing them from Hypollite Jasmin. The window slid open a few inches.

"Where is the little black box, monsieur Jasmin? We want to look at T.V."

"Not worth it, mademoiselle. We'll be there in a few minutes."

"To a villa near Cannes? That will take half an hour at least."

"Not Cannes, monsieur. We go to the rendezvous in Nice. At the Roman ruins in Cimiez."

Why Nice? The Assistant Secretary felt a new uneasiness.

"That will be interesting," Gabrielle said. "The Romans

were everywhere. Did you know that? Even in Paris you have the *arènes de Lutèce* on the Left Bank. The Romans had fine baths for the public, one bath for the men and another for the women. Much better than the bathing establishments in the Seine, although the separation of the sexes was regrettable. In Nîmes there is a great Roman amphitheater where today they fight the bulls."

The car moved silently along the Moyenne Corniche. Villefranche disappeared. Minutes later they were above Nice and the lights of the Promenade des Anglais stretching in a gentle crescent toward the airport, the Atlantic, home. One bright cluster of lights would be the Negresco where Dr. Monzon was blown up. And somewhere in the city was the *traficante* Roque Amador and his white Rolls-Royce. The Assistant Secretary pondered the Colombian's possible interest in himself.

Could the Grand Patron have sold him to Amador?

He tapped the dividing glass until it slid open.

"It doesn't make sense, monsieur Jasmin. If the Grand Patron is turning us over to the President-for-Life, why not take us to him?"

Jasmin said nothing.

"Drive us to the American consulate in Nice and I will guarantee you two million francs."

Jasmin shook his head.

"Money is nothing, monsieur. Loyalty to the President-for-Life and to the Grand Patron is everything."

The window closed.

"Two million francs," Gabrielle said. "That would be excessive."

The car wound through narrow streets and turned north onto the Boulevard de Cimiez, a broad avenue climbing toward the hills. They passed the lush gardens and dark mansions once occupied by the Victorian nobles and the millionaires who followed Queen Victoria to her winter sojourn and the massive Hotel Regina. The wide avenue was deserted. Behind them was the Musée Chagall, the railroad station, hotels, the American Consulate, the Negresco.

They turned onto a smaller street, slowed, stopped. On their left were the moonlit ruins, ahead was the small building that was the museum. It was three-fifteen. Barbed wire separated the road from recent excavations. A lonely place for a loyal Haitian subject to meet an envoy of the President-for-Life. Hypollite Jasmin lit a cigarette.

The Assistant Secretary tapped on the partition. The glass moved a few inches.

"Have you asked yourself why you aren't taking us all the way to Cannes? Why should the President's man have to come thirty kilometers, you only ten?"

"For your safety, monsieur. And yours, mademoiselle. Once in the President's hands, nothing can touch you. In a few minutes you will be in the President's car."

"You are quite sure it's the President's envoy you are meeting?"

"Of course."

"You may be right, monsieur Jasmin. However, I have to suggest something a little disagreeable. If the Grand Patron wanted to turn us over to the Colombian *trafficeur* Roque Amador, wouldn't this be a good place to do it? No witnesses. No one would ever know what happened here."

"That's crazy, monsieur. What an idea!"

"Yes," Gabrielle said. "That's stupid."

"Just consider for a moment, Monsieur Jasmin. Remember your life is in question too, not just ours."

"My life?"

"Let us assume for the moment it is Amador's man we are meeting. Or even Amador himself. Once he has taken us over, what are you?"

"I'm nothing. I get in the car and go back to Cap Ferrat."

"On the contrary, you have been a witness. You have been a witness dangerous to both the Grand Patron and Roque Amador. If you were to tell the police what you saw . . ."

With a flick of a thumb and finger, possibly without even thinking, Hypollite Jasmin turned on the ignition. The long car came quietly to life.

"I would never tell the police."

"Amador and the Grand Patron would have an equal interest in you as a witness. In my opinion you would be shot. By Amador here or by the Grand Patron back at Cap Ferrat. Why take the risk? Why not take us into Nice and then go back to La Morinière and your comfortable chateau."

The car moved slowly toward the rendevous beyond the museum, then circled back.

"I have decided there is no need for a witness." The door locks snapped up. "Get out at once and walk hand in hand to the museum and fifty meters beyond it. Stay there until the envoy of the President comes for you. If you move away from the steps you will be shot. I will be watching you from the car."

They did as they were told. They had no choice. A pale light showed somewhere in the interior of the museum building. In the clear moonlight they could read a sign saying that the museum was closed, both the archeological portion and the portion devoted to Matisse.

The first time they looked back they could see the Mercedes half-hidden by the only large tree at the eastern periphery of the ruins. The next time they looked back it was gone.

"He has fled," Gabrielle said. "He is a coward."

"He wants to go on living."

The Assistant Secretary looked for a bell at the entrance to the museum. In the museum there would certainly be a telephone, also a guardian. If they could raise the guard they might get to a telephone, call the American Consulate, hide in the guard's quarters until help came. He rang the bell again and pounded on the door using his left hand.

It was three-twenty-five.

"The guardian sleeps," Gabrielle said.

The distant lights of the city cast a pale curving glow above the trees and dark houses at the base of the ruins. Nearer were the lights of an approaching car, followed at some distance by a second car.

The Assistant Secretary was terrified.

Across the street were the moonlit ruins with their many habitations of the dead. Among them there should be places to hide...

"Come on, follow me."

Fifty feet or so up the road there was a break in the enclosure where further excavations were underway. They went through it and stumbled into a deep ditch that had brick walls and a smooth stone floor. A cat screeched and leaped out of the ditch. It stood at the lip of the excavation and stared down at them, hissing. Malevolent eyes shone in the moonlight.

"That is not a house cat," Gabrielle said.

They followed the ditch to an opening that led to the heart of the ruins. A single high column rose white and menacing above uneven walls and two columns broken off near the base. A narrow stone conduit that might have been an aqueduct led toward broken walls in the direction of the Boulevard de Cimiez, Nice, safety. They followed it. They were well hidden in the darkness of the conduit but could not see what had happened to the two cars.

The ditch opened into a dark deep rectangular space of shadowed walls. On top of the walls were more cats.

"I think we are in one of the baths of the Romans," Gabrielle said. "There is no way to tell whether it is for the men or for the women, this bath."

He touched her elbow in a gesture meant to be forgiving, even affectionate. He was glad not to be alone in these ruins.

"You should have your head examined. I'll arrange for it if we ever get free." He put his hand on her right shoulder. "In another life I think I would be in love with you."

"Eventually, why not now?"

"What?"

"That's the advertisement for a funeral establishment in Paris. 'Eventually, why not now'?"

He kissed her.

They climbed a small flight of stairs and saw, alarmingly close, the dimmed lights of the two cars at the entrance of the museum. They had gone in circles, groping in the ruins.

"All right," he said. "We have to get out of here. Down this way."

Ten minutes later they were at the base of the ruins. The Assistant Secretary's trousers were torn, one of Gabrielle's knees was bleeding. They were covered with bruises.

The long wide stretch of the Boulevard de Cimiez lay ahead, sloping down toward the city in a solitude bordered by villas and their thick gardens. He led her through a break in the hedge and into the first of the gardens. There were high palms and a small grove of olive trees with leaves that were silvery in the moonlight.

"We'll make a run for it down the boulevard, but keep inside the hedges. If the cars come just lie flat unless there's something to hide behind."

They began to work their way down through the gardens.

They had gone perhaps a quarter of a mile when they heard them descending from the area of the ruins, then saw them through a break in the hedge. A dark two-door sedan with a diesel rattling, followed by a silently gliding white Rolls-Royce convertible. The top had been raised so that nothing could be seen but the glow of a cigarette or cigar. A powerful spotlight from the Rolls raked the hedges and the gates to the villa grounds, first the east side of the street, then the west. The cars continued on down toward the city, the spotlight playing on the hedges. Then they were gone.

"If they come back just lie down. Don't move at all."

It was five minutes to four. The cars did not return.

"They are discouraged," Gabrielle said.

"I think they'll be back. Maybe they've gone on to Cap Ferrat to wipe out the Grand Patron for not showing up."

"Those nice children Ti Roro and La Séductrice, will they be orphans again?"

"Very likely."

"And the poor maître? Will they put him back in the cage next to the nuns and take away his clothes?"

"That's the least of my worries," he said. "Maybe they won't be back but let's don't chance it. We'll stay inside the hedges. That spotlight could pick us up from a mile off."

They worked their way down through the gardens. They stumbled into ditches and tripped over boulders, brushed aside nettled branches, climbed over fences. Twice when there were stone walls it was necessary to go out onto the open exposure of the boulevard. They walked down it rapidly, alert for lights returning or the sound of cars. But there were no sounds of cars, only the screech and heavy rumble of freight cars on the train tracks not far ahead. And only the scattered lights of the city center and the curving bright necklace of the promenade.

They came to a massive modern building just off the boulevard, the Musée Chagall. A narrow alley offered a good hiding place where he could wait for the Consulate to pick him up with complete discretion. It all had to be as quiet as possible.

Near the gate and bus stop was a curbside telephone booth.

But he had no telephone charge card, no tokens, no money, no wallet. Neither had she. Gabrielle reached into the cup for returned tokens. It was empty. She pushed all the buttons but there was no response.

"I will go to a café and telephone the police."

"How can you telephone if you don't have any money or any tokens?"

"They will give me tokens," she said. "All I need."

"I guess you might as well try." He looked down at her, wanting to remember the color of her eyes. In the dark he couldn't tell, and it was very likely he was seeing her for the last time. He did not want her to go to prison. No, he did not want that at all. "Listen to me carefully. You must telephone the American Consulate here in Nice and tell them who I am and have them wake up the Consul. Tell them exactly where I will be, just here by the entrance to the Musée Chagall. I'll stay out of sight until I see them come. The Consulate can take it from there. Tell them to keep the reporters away."

"Why not the French police?"

"Try the Consulate first. If you can't get through, go ahead and call the police."

"That is all?"

Was it all? He touched her chin with the index finger of his good hand. Even here her skin was wonderfully soft. He did not want her to go.

"You've come a long way, haven't you, for a poor girl from the provinces?"

"Why do you say that?"

"Do we shake hands or kiss goodbye?"

"You think I will run away, monsieur? That is ridiculous. They would certainly find me sooner or later. Besides, I want to be admitted to the United States. I will return and stay with you."

"I don't want you to go to prison." He tried to make light of it. "You would corrupt all the guards."

"You will tell the police I too was a victim."

She kissed him and walked away in the direction of the railroad and the lights and the cafés with their telephones. It was a quick, almost perfunctory kiss, a soft brush of one cheek that implied she would soon return. For a greeting or farewell the two cheeks were obligatory. And yet it seemed to him she was walking out of his life. He listened with a hollow sickness to the diminishing clicks on the pavement. Already she was only a shadow among shadows.

SHE INTENDED TO RETURN. So she told herself, walking briskly past the first dark shuttered shops, the gloomy apartments and the cafés long since closed for the night, the railroad bridge only a few hundred meters ahead. *I will explain to them all the circumstances, the Assistant Secretary will defend me, it will be at the maximum two or three years of unpleasantness, not Devil's Island anyway.* Nevertheless the stricken faces of several men and two women intruded, looking away from the television cameras, condemned for offences against the security of the state. Being led away in handcuffs. Ten years, twenty years, life.

Directly ahead and across from the gloomy station was a café evidently open all night. She went in. The bartender and an old man in a poorly fitting overcoat were shooting dice. He must be ill, the poor man, to wear an overcoat on a summer night.

She exchanged greetings with the two. The bartender took in her bloody knee and the scratches on her face. He raised his shoulders, turned up his hands, shook his head. *That's life,* he seemed to be saying.

"A friend beat you up?"

"A thug. First he took my money, then he beat me up."

The bartender whistled twice, recognizing he would be asked for a free drink. He reached for his towel and wiped the bar.

"What will it be? Coffee or a glass of wine. Not both."

"A little glass of white, please."

The old man put a coin on the bar.

"It's my treat, this one. Any time for a pretty young girl."

She gave his thin hand a squeeze. It was a kind hand, not at all like the maître's skeletal claw.

"I need a token for the telephone. I must call for help."

"Give her a token," the old man said.

The bartender went to the cash register and returned with a token.

"You don't look like a tramp," he said. "You live in Nice?"

"Only visiting."

She went down the stairs to the the dimly lit area of the telephone and the toilet. She called the operator, explained that it was an emergency and asked to be connected with the American Consulate.

"They will be asleep at this hour of the night, the Americans. Everyone should be asleep."

"Nevertheless I beg you to try. It's a tragic situation, an American in great trouble."

Eventually the Consulate responded, an angry French voice. It told her to call in the morning, not before nine o'clock.

"A man, an American diplomat, is in danger of losing his life. Wake the Consul. You will regret it if the man is killed, you will be responsible."

"You sound deranged. Are you drunk, mademoiselle?"

"I beg you."

Five minutes later the Consul himself was on the line. Thank God he knew French.

"What's this about a diplomat?"

She cupped her mouth and dropped her voice to a whisper. It was important not to be overheard by them, the two men upstairs.

"I am with the kidnapped Assistant Secretary of State. Mr. Randall. He is in great danger of death from the Colombian with the Rolls."

"I don't believe you. Who told you to call me?"

"Mr. Randall did. I am the femme de chambre Gabrielle Soubiran, also the victim of a kidnapping."

There was a long silence. The Consul was breathing heavily. Another old man, perhaps?

"Where are you?"

Her voice rose in exasperation.

"In a café across from the station. But it's not that, the

question. The Assistant Secretary is hiding himself near the entrance to the Musée Chagall. You know where that is, the Musée Chagall?''

Another silence. Fortunately the operator who had arranged this call was listening. Otherwise there would be a demand for more tokens.

"I don't know what to believe," the Consul said.

"What do you have to lose, sir?"

"My sleep."

"And will you sleep better, then, after the Assistant Secretary is dead?"

She was alarmed to realize that she had shouted.

"Calm down, mademoiselle. What's the name of that café?"

"It's the only café that's open, across from the station."

She was still talking too loud.

"Don't you move from that café. I'll get the police, and the CIA."

"Not the café. The entrance to the Musée Chagall."

"Which entrance?"

"By the boulevard."

The two men were standing at the head of the stairs. They were looking down at her in astonishment.

"Is it true what you were saying. It's really you, the femme de chambre of the Meurice?"

She pushed past them and looked at herself in the mirror behind the bar. What a fright! And she had nothing with her, not even lipstick.

"Will you give me another glass? A white wine this time, if possible."

"The flics will be here any minute. Better have a shot of something stronger."

The old man put his cold hand on hers. His watery blue eyes were compassionate.

"You don't look like a criminal," he said. "You look like someone I knew long ago."

"You can't tell by looks," the bartender said.

"We heard everything," the old man said. "You told them where to go for the kidnapped diplomat. Why should you go to prison? Everyone has made mistakes, me first of all. Finish your drink and take off."

He reached for his wallet and opened it. Nothing. He emptied the pockets of his overcoat. In the second pocket was a thin black change purse. He gave her two ten-franc coins.

"Get a taxi at the station. Go down by the port, go into the Old Town. You are young, you have a life to live."

She kissed the bony hand.

"I will remember you all my life, monsieur."

"You are an accomplice," the bartender said to the old man. "It's not without danger, what you're doing."

"Let them arrest me."

She shook hands with both men and walked quickly to the line of taxis. There were only two. She woke up the driver of the first one.

"What time is it?" he asked. "Where are you going?"

Where? Monte Carlo and the Hotel de Paris, where she might find employment as a femme de chambre? The beach at Juan-les-Pins was said to be the best, but Cannes had more attractions, nightclubs and good restaurants. It was something she had thought about for some time, one of those beaches where one sunned oneself in the nude. But would it not rather be some horrible estaminet in a miserable African country, most likely a prostitute through no fault of her own? And what had happened to her plans for a good job in Washington, in that hotel the Assistant Secretary said was the best?

"What's the matter with you, little one? Where do you want to go?"

"To the Musée Chagall," she said.

"You're crazy. The museum at this hour?"

"I am meeting a friend." Why shouldn't she say her lover? "A secret relationship."

The driver laughed.

"After that I take you to a hotel? I can recommend an excellent two-star hotel, very cheap."

"That would be nice. But we will have a car."

But at the Musée Chagall all was darkness, no police cars, no Assistant Secretary. She got out of the taxi.

"There's nothing here," the driver said. "Get back in."

The Assistant Secretary stepped out of the darkness. He hugged her, ran his fingers through her hair and pulled her head back. He kissed her on the mouth, gently.

"You came back."

"They are coming," she said. "They connect me with the Consul who at first does not believe me. Now they are coming, the police and your CIA."

The taxi driver had been listening. The words *police* and *CIA* made him uneasy. He raced his engine.

"I'm taking off. I don't get involved with these affairs."

"Just a moment," Randall said. He ran his fingers through her hair again. How soft it was. No, he did not want her to go to prison. "My friend is coming with you."

But the taxi had already gone.

"He is afraid of the police, that one," Gabrielle said. "You wanted me to run away? If I run away I will never get to the United States. That is what I want, to visit the United

States. All the cities, also the natural spectacles, Niagara Falls, for instance."

The lights of several cars approached. Then the cars were there. Two French police vans, a third car with the Americans. They were caught in the lights of the three cars. There was much handshaking with the Assistant Secretary.

Two policemen were holding Gabrielle.

"You are Gabrielle Soubiran?" It was a brisk young American in a dark suit.

"Yes. But I answer no more questions."

"Take it easy on her," the Assistant Secretary said to the policemen. "You see that she didn't run away. She has helped me."

"Don't make any statements, Mr. Randall," one of the Americans said.

"Come along," one of the policemen said to Gabrielle, pulling her by the elbow. "It's finished, your little dance."

They put her in one of the police vans. She waved to him before the door closed.

The young American introduced a disheveled older man in a rumpled shirt and no tie. And gray hairs. He looked very tired.

"This is the man who really found you, Mr. Randall," the young American said. "Gordon Seymour, cultural attaché at the Embassy."

"Cultural attaché? How the hell did you get into this?"

"It's a long story," Gordon said.

The Assistant Secretary measured the two men, the CIA chief Trent, the oddball cultural attaché Seymour. He decided the older man was the better bet.

"I don't want her kicked around, Seymour. She tried to help me. In a way it was all a mistake and she was a victim too. Be sure you do everything you can to protect her."

The cultural attaché looked sympathetic.

"That could give you a little trouble with the media, Mr. Randall. It might be misinterpreted."

"I'm not talking to the media," the Assistant Secretary said. "Make sure you don't give them any ideas."

THE MEDIA WERE THERE WHEN the Air Force plane took off in the first morning light, shouting questions: *"How about the French babe? What's the story with the femme de chambre? What's your comment on the sex and chains pix? Are you going to resign?"* But the Assistant Secretary's only words, spoken first in English then in careful French, were to thank the Minister of the Interior, the Minister of Justice, and the various French intelligence and police services for their successful search and rescue, in which they were assisted by American personnel. He was wearing a hat that concealed his hair, but obligingly held up his bandaged hand for the photographers.

THE INTERROGATION OF GABRIELLE SOUBIRAN had already begun. Gordon checked in at police headquarters later in the morning, only to be referred to a private villa on the Boulevard Victor Hugo. There he was the subject of much friendly curiosity as the *attaché culturel* who had shown himself both courageous and intuitive and able to speak French correctly. But he was not permitted to attend the interrogation. He reserved a room for Gabrielle at the Sofitel Splendid in the next block, then decided to stay there himself for an hour's nap. He had slept only two hours in twenty-four but could not sleep now. In a waking dream he stared at the ceiling and meditated on the extraordinary behavior of the Assistant Secretary and on the decidedly attractive Gabrielle. He got up and at ten o'clock saw himself in a delayed newscast from the airport, an oddly unprofessional figure among the French officials and policemen and the men from the Consulate and the CIA.

At eleven, when he returned to the villa, the police were showing signs of exasperation. Even before he could sit down two sweating men with shirt collars unbuttoned emerged from the interrogation room to take a break. One of them was laughing, the other was swearing softly.

"She is crazy," the first said. "A fantastic who invents lies without effort or premeditation. Says she will tell the full story only in Washington."

"She belongs in the theater," the other said. "What she needs is a good spanking."

"She will get it before I'm through," said the first.

Gordon got up from his chair, where he was reading the *Figaro*, to remind them that this was an affair that concerned the United States, and that the American public would not tolerate mistreatment of a suspect in an affair involving an American diplomat.

A half-hour later a third interrogator emerged, mopping his brow. His hair was disheveled, his sleeves were rolled up over hairy arms.

"She wants a lawyer, also coffee, brioches with butter and strawberry jam and a bottle of Rose de Provence. Otherwise she won't speak. I told her what to do with the bottle."

Ten minutes later, he took in a mug of coffee and a demi-baguette and a small pot of jam. Also a bottle of vin ordinaire.

Shortly after noon the three interrogators came out, followed by Gabrielle. Her hair was in disarray, her eyeshadow was smudged. Her left eye might have been blackened by a blow. She had the look of a woman who had been slapped, browbeaten, raped. But she was free pending filing of charges and a call from the juge d'instruction. She was not to leave Nice.

"I'm not going anywhere. I don't have any money."

"She has a room at the Sofitel Splendid," Gordon said. "She will be there when you need her."

Gabrielle gave him a surprised glance. Tiny furrows appeared in the forehead still damp from the lights of the interrogation room. Her brown eyes rose to his gray hair, then fell to his scuffed shoes.

"But who are you, monsieur?"

"I am the cultural attaché of the United States Embassy in Paris."

"Ô là là!"

An enigmatic response, Gordon thought. Little more than a whisper, but one that combined bewilderment and pleasure.

"I was deputized to look after you."

A small lie, after all, "deputized" was not exactly the right word. But he had acted independently for nine days and one more wouldn't hurt.

"You will take me to the Hotel Sofitel Splendid, monsieur? I would have preferred the Negresco."

"It's not the Meurice or the Negresco. But there's a pool on the eighth floor and a great view."

"Very good. That will be all right. Do you like to swim?"

Her manner had brightened considerably by the time they left the police villa. They walked the long block to the Sofitel Splendid. She tugged at her clothes as they walked, squirming. Her heels clicked on the pavement.

"I have a horror of the police," she said. "But in the last hour they were much more agreeable. Tell me frankly, monsieur. Are you also going to interrogate me?" She went on, not waiting for an answer. "This is the Boulevard Victor Hugo, named after the great poet who also wrote novels. *Notre Dame de Paris. Les Misérables.* Some others. That is the Hotel Malmaison, where I stayed on one of my vacations with a student from the Sorbonne. Excellent, but more modest than the Sofitel Splendid."

At the reception desk she shook hands briskly with the clerk. Two men with cameras stepped out from behind a partition and took pictures. Gabrielle grinned, then stuck out her tongue. Her appearance had improved immeasurably in the five minutes since they left the police station. Gordon accompanied her as far as the elevator. She had no baggage, but a mouche would show her the room. A second mouche approached, evidently wanting to go along.

She turned to Gordon, smiling.

"You are also in this hotel, monsieur?"

"No, I'm at the Negresco. You can call me if there's anything you want. Mr. Randall asked me to look after you."

"He said that? How very nice! He is a man of many good qualities." Her eyes filled with tears, but she quickly rubbed them away. "At the moment I want a massage, then a swim in the pool on the eighth floor, followed by the hairdresser. Will the United States pay for all that?" She frowned. "Please accompany me to the room. My spirit has had many shocks, I am still afraid."

They went to her room, preceded by the two mouches. One unlocked the door.

"You'll be all right now," Gordon said.

She held out her hand, gave his a friendly squeeze.

"I thank you for your help, monsieur." She looked over her shoulder at the two mouches bustling about in the bedroom, then back at him. "Do you know the city of Nice?"

"Not really. I was here a long time ago. In the war."

"The war? Which war?"

Her lips moved, as though counting. Her brown eyes measured him.

"I know the city from several vacations," she went on. "The Palais de la Mediterranée, the museums, the attractions. I also know the best restaurants, both the luxurious places and the good modest ones. It is a city where one is well nourished, Nice."

He was fascinated with the wisdom of years but as tongue-tied as an adolescent.

"So I have heard," he managed.

"I will show you around, monsieur. You are the cultural attaché, so we will go first to the museums, then to the attractions. How long will you be in Nice?"